PRAISE FOR CYNTHIA D'ALBA

Praise for Cynthia D'Alba

"Highly recommend to all fans of hot cowboys, firefighters, and romance."

—Emily, Goodreads on Saddles and Soot

"Outstanding love story."

—Avid Reader, Amazon on *A Cowboy's Seduction*

"This book was fun and I loved every page of it."

—Connie, Goodreads on *A Cowboy's Seduction*

"This author does an amazing job of keeping readers on their toes while maintaining a natural flow to the story."

—RT Book Reviews on *Texas Hustle*

"Cynthia D'Alba's *Texas Fandango* from Samhain lets readers enjoy the sensual fun in the sun [...] This latest offering gives readers a sexy escape and a reason to seek out D'Alba's earlier titles."

—Library Journal Reviews on *Texas Fandango*

"[...] inclusions that stand out for all the right reasons is Cynthia D'Alba's clever *Backstage Pass*"

—Publisher's Weekly on *Backstage Pass* in *Cowboy Heat*

"*Texas Two Step* kept me on an emotional roller coaster [...] *Texas Two Step* is an emotionally charged romance, with well-developed characters and an engaging secondary cast. A quarter of the way into the book I added Ms. D'Alba to my auto-buys."

—5 Stars and Recommended Read, Guilty Pleasure Book Reviews on *Texas Two Step*

"I loved this book. The characters came alive. They had

depth, interest and completeness. But more than the romance and sex which were great, there are connections with family and friends which makes this story so much more than a story about two people."

—Night Owl Romance 5 STARS! A TOP PICK *on Texas Bossa Nova*

"Wow, what an amazing romance novel. *Texas Lullaby* is an impassioned, well-written book with a genuine love story that took hold of my heart and soul from the very beginning."

—LJT, Amazon Reviews, on *Texas Lullaby*

"An emotional, complex and beautiful story of love and life and how it can all change in a heartbeat."

—DiDi, Guilty Pleasures Book Reviews on *Texas Lullaby*

"*TEXAS LULLABY* is a refreshing departure from the traditional romance plot in that it features an already committed couple."

—Tangled Hearts Book Reviews on *Texas Lullaby*

"A great read with just the right amount of steamy sexual tension and a HEA!"

—D. Yochum, Just The Write Touch, on Cadillac Cowboy

TEXAS JUSTICE

CYNTHIA D'ALBA

Texas Justice

By Cynthia D'Alba

Copyright © 2016 Cynthia D'Alba and Riante, Inc.

Print ISBN: 978-0-9982650-4-9

Digital ISBN: 978-0-9982650-5-6

Cover Artist: Elle James

Editor: Heidi Moore

I can honestly say that without the support of the D'Alba Diamonds, my street team, this book would never have been finished. They've carried me over the past months as I've struggled with newly diagnosed breast cancer. This writing gig would be a much lonelier life without them. Thank you, Diamonds.

Thank you also to Eileen McCall and Ruth Smithson for all the reading and suggestions you did for this book. Hugs to Angie Campbell for all her edits and corrections. Any mistakes are mine and mine alone.

And without the support of my fellow Cowboy Justice authors, I would have quit. But they were always there, supporting me, encouraging me. Thank you, ladies.

CHAPTER ONE

"Sorry, ma'am. I'm gonna have to frisk you."

"But, Sheriff, I didn't do anything," Tess Sweeney said, rapidly batting her eyelashes. "I swear."

She dragged out the last two words in the best damned Scarlet O'Hara imitation she could do. The corners of his mouth twitched for a minute before his face transformed into a stern expression.

"Spread 'em," he ordered, deepening his voice into a growl.

"If I don't, are you going to pistol whip me?" She made a point of sticking out her lower lip in a pout.

"No, ma'am, but I might have to use my big nightstick on you."

Tess squealed with laughter. "Has that line ever worked?"

Tess looked up into the steel-gray eyes of Kyle Monroe. He gave her a smile that sent her heart racing. Sexual energy flared, melting her insides.

"Nope, but a man's gotta have hope." He brushed the back of his fingers along her cheek. She pressed her face into his touch. His eyes darkened with desire. Every cell in her body lit up.

"Have I told you how beautiful you are?"

A huge lump formed in her throat. Too thin and too plain as a child, she'd never had much attention from boys. By the time she'd reached high school, she'd developed large breasts, a narrow waist, and hips that swung when she walked. But inside, she was still that skinny, ugly little girl nobody picked for their kickball team.

Tess's elbows sank into the mattress as she arched her back, crushing her breasts against his chest. She savored the feel of the rough hair there against her sensitive nipples. "You might have mentioned it once or twice over dinner." She ran her tongue around his nipple and caught it between her teeth, tugging gently on the rigid flesh.

He caught her head between his hands, holding her against his chest. His deep-throated moan told her how much he loved the rasp of her tongue on his flesh.

Moving up his body, she kissed and nibbled until she reached his lower lip. She sucked it between her lips and then looked at him. "But for now, less talk. More action." She raked her taut nipples through his chest hair again.

"Yes, ma'am," he said as he rolled her onto her back and worked his way down her neck.

Beside her right ear her cell phone vibrated on the oak bedside table. It pulsated twice more, followed by loud gonging.

"Argh," she moaned, dropping her arms out to her sides. Did she have to get a call the first time she was in bed with this incredibly sexy man? Of course she did.

"Don't answer it," he said, tightening his arms around her like a steel band.

"You know I have to." She glanced at the clock and

sighed. One a.m. Nobody got good news at this hour. "I'm on call. No choice."

Tess kissed the tip of his nose and slipped from the mattress. She hurried around the bed and grabbed her cell phone off the table. "Dr. Sweeney."

She glanced back at the man in her bed and wanted to weep at being on call. He'd scooted up until his back rested against her headboard. His chest was a rock-hard display of muscle and sinew that begged to be touched...and she wanted to stroke it so bad her fingers itched. His eyes were on her, listening as she took her call from the emergency department.

She forced her attention back to the call.

"Dr. Sweeney. This is John Tanner from St. Michael's Hospital."

"Oh, hi, John. What'd you have?"

"MVA. Young boy. Thrown from the car upon collision."

"Uh-huh. How old?"

"Five, but quite small for his age."

She opened the bedside table drawer and pulled out a sheet of paper to jot notes as the Emergency Department physician continued his report. "Okay. Have you already done the type and cross for blood?"

"Sent it off to the lab a couple of minutes ago. The parents say they think he is O positive, which would be great. I'm sure the blood bank will have that."

"Great. Parents are there at the hospital then?"

"Yep. Last name's Lloyd. Hold on." Papers rattled. "Um, parents are Preston and Constance."

"Preston Lloyd, our district attorney?" Her chest squeezed her heart.

"Yeah."

"Great, just great." She blew out a long breath and tapped a dozen ink splotches on the paper with her pen. Lloyd was a first-class asshole. She'd done a first-class job avoiding him in the two years she'd lived in Diamond Lakes, Texas.

"And I have to tell you, Tess. He reeks of alcohol."

"What about his wife?"

"She didn't seem to be injured in the accident."

"I don't give a shit about either of them. They're not my patients, but I do need them sober enough to sign the damn surgery permit for their son."

"Well, she was a little incoherent when they came in, but I think she's more frantic about her son than alcohol impaired. Him? I wouldn't let him sign anything. I can't be sure he's clear-headed enough to give informed consent."

"Fine. I'll trust your judgment on that. Get the consent signed for an exploratory lap and call the OR team in. Make sure the blood bank stays two units ahead on packed cells. Oh, and, John, see if you can badger radiology into fresh pictures for the OR. I'd like to have a better idea of what the hell I'm getting into before I cut the kid open."

"Will do, Tess."

Tess slammed the phone back on the dresser. "Sono-fabitch thinks laws don't apply to him. Never has thought about anybody but himself. Asshole," she muttered as she stomped across the room. She jerked open a drawer, snatched out fresh underwear, a pair of fresh scrubs, and marched into the bathroom. As she shut the door, she heard Kyle's phone ringing. She wasn't surprised the deputy on duty would call the sheriff when the county district attorney was involved in an accident where there were injuries.

Sheriff Kyle Monroe was stomping his feet into a pair of cowboy boots when Tess walked out of the bathroom. In the time she'd been in there, he'd gotten dressed.

"You don't need to drive me," she said.

"Wasn't planning to. Our district attorney and his family were hit by a teenage driver who happens to be one of the

Worthington boys. Texas State Police will take it, but the sergeant on duty thought I might want in the loop on this. What a mess this'll be."

She frowned. "Not the first time one of Judge Worthington's boys been in trouble, is it?" She gave him a quick kiss. "I've gotta go. It's quite a drive from here."

"I'll run blue lights to the hospital. Stay on my tail and we'll be there in less than ten minutes."

"Appreciate it, Kyle."

He missed his time estimation by two minutes. Eight minutes after they left her house, Dr. Tess Sweeney blew through the ambulance bay doors and raced down the emergency department hallway of St. Michael's Hospital. The doors to trauma room two were open, and she glanced in. Blood-soaked towels and four-by-four gauze pads littered the floor, along with paper and boxes from medical supplies. An empty IV bag lay among the waste, its tubing curled like a snake.

Opening the door to the nurses' station, she saw Martha Womack, the shift charge nurse.

"Martha. Where's the Lloyd child?" Tess knew she sounded brusque and harried, but she'd have to apologize to Martha another time. She was losing precious time to save her patient.

Martha Womack, a gray-haired woman well into her fifties, looked over her shoulder. "Hey, Tess. Upstairs in the OR. Once Tanner got the blood pressure stabilized, the OR staff picked him up. Tanner went along since we have nothing down here needing his attention at the moment. He wanted to have a word with the anesthesiologist."

"Great. Where are the parents? John get the consent form signed?"

"Got it. Parents went with the child during transport. I think they were going to the chapel."

"Good. I'll talk to them after the surgery. Thanks." Tess raced for the elevators.

———

WHEN TESS HAD TURNED in to the hospital's physician parking, Kyle had tapped his siren once and flown on past. If he hurried, he might get to the crash site before the state police. Sure, his guys would secure the scene while they waited for state to swoop in and take over the investigation. Most of the time, it would have bugged the crap out of him to have the state tromping around his territory, but not so much tonight. The reality was he didn't care much for their county district attorney. Lloyd was arrogant with an elitist view of the world. They'd butted heads on more than one occasion.

Still, he didn't wish harm to the man's son.

An accident investigation team from the state police was already on site when he arrived. Blue strobe lights from a gaggle of law enforcement vehicles lit up the surrounding trees and road. In front of his SUV, a Texas state trooper walked with a flashlight along dark tire skid marks. Shards of broken glass glinted under the beam and Kyle could hear the crunch of glass under the trooper's heavy boots. He recognized the man by his stride and nodded to himself.

"Gruber," he called as he exited his truck.

The man turned and raised his arm, bringing the daylight brightness from his flashlight directly into Kyle's face. Kyle shielded his eyes.

"Monroe," the trooper said. "Come out to see the clusterfuck?"

Kyle shook his head with a knowing sigh. An accident involving two prominent families with a serious injury was nothing but a logistical nightmare for whatever office drew the short straw. Tonight, since it was the county district attorney, the state police had the honors.

The two men shook hands. "Clusterfuck is probably as accurate a description as any," Kyle said. "Thought I'd drop by and see if you guys needed anything from us."

"We're good," Shade Gruber said. "Your guys did a great job securing the scene, with one exception."

"Oh? What'd they miss?"

"We can't find the boy's car seat. Lloyd said his son was ejected from the car seat when it flew out of his car with the child still inside."

Kyle pursed his lips. "That's interesting. What about Lloyd's car? Was there damage to the seatbelts?"

"Nope. Lloyd said his wife never got the hang of putting the seat in correctly."

"What did she say?"

"Not much. She was too distraught to give us any help. Both of them left in the ambulance with their son."

"Alcohol?"

"Who? Lloyd or the judge's kid?"

"Either. Both. Whatever. Just thinking out loud."

Gruber shook his head. "Worthington kid's a little slurry and shook up. Second ambulance left with him right behind the Lloyds. Preston Lloyd smelled like undiluted bourbon, but there was a broken bottle in his car. Said his wife was carrying it home from a fundraiser and it broke in the crash."

"I'll let you get back to work. I'll check in with my deputies and be on my way. Let me know if you do decide you need anything from us."

"Will do. Thanks."

Gruber went back to measuring the skid marks. Kyle walked over to a fresh-faced deputy. New guy hired recently.

"Adams," Kyle said, reading the name on the officer's nametag.

"Sir." The deputy, who must have been all of twenty-four, straightened.

"Appreciate the heads- up about Lloyd," Kyle said.

"Yes, sir."

"Give me a quick report of what happened once you arrived on the scene."

"The cars were where you see them. The Lloyds were out of their car and on the ground next to their son. The teenager was out of his truck, sort of swaying and holding on the hood, as though he was using it to hold himself upright. As soon as Lloyd identified himself, I contacted the state police while Anderson—" he tilted his head toward his partner near the creek, "—looked for the child's car seat."

"I know this is not our accident to cover, but could you do a write up for me tomorrow with all the details you have? Probably won't ever need it, but if I've learned anything over the years, it's when lawyers are involved, have all the facts you can documented while they're still fresh."

"Yes, sir."

The sheriff clapped the deputy on the shoulder. "See you tomorrow. Have dispatch notify me if you need me back out here tonight."

CHAPTER TWO

The hospital elevator doors slid open on level two and Tess rushed out, banging through the double surgery doors.

"Dr. Sweeney," a scrub tech called from the end of the hall. "We're in OR three."

Tess sighed. Operating room three was typically used for the worst cases. Quickly donning a hat, mask, and eye covers, she followed the tech through the doors to the OR suites. After popping open a soap-infused brush, she placed her hands beneath the motion-sensor water faucet and went to work on them.

The scrub tech moved alongside Tess. "We've got him on the table. We were lucky that Dr. Madison was in Labor and Delivery putting in an epidural."

Tess nodded. Dr. Guy Madison was an excellent anesthesiologist, exactly the person she wanted for a complicated case. Glancing through the OR window, she spotted him chatting with Sue Johnson, the circulating nurse, while she prepped a very small abdomen.

"Got some current films?" Tess asked, continuing to coat her hands and arms in white foamy lather.

"Yes, ma'am." She pointed to the large digital viewer on the wall in the operating room. Tess studied it through the OR window as she scrubbed and shook her head. Blood surrounded most of the vital organs.

"I know," Nina said. "Even I can see the blood. The kid's lucky to have made it this far."

Tess rinsed her hands and then held them up so excess water dripped off her elbows. "Poor kid. Thrown from the car. No way was he in a booster seat."

She backed into the OR and accepted the sterile towel offered by the first scrub tech. "Morning, Pete," she said, drying her hands.

"Morning, Doc," he answered, his voice grave. He held up a sterile gown and she shoved her arms through the sleeves. He pulled latex gloves over her hands.

Her patient's body had already been draped with blue sterile sheets. At her first look at her patient, her heart sank. The normally pink skin was pasty white. The small chest and abdomen were the only parts of his tiny body visible to her. A unit of blood was dripping into his system.

"Guy," Tess said. "Good to have you here. You got our boy ready?"

"Morning, Tess. He's as stable as I can get him, which isn't saying much I'm afraid."

She nodded and shifted her eyes toward the sterile-clad scrub nurse beside her. "Scalpel," she said, holding out her hand.

Surgery was a disaster from the start. No amount of suction or copious volume of sponges could control the hemorrhage. Tess repaired, stitched, and removed as much of the organ damage as she could, but within the first thirty minutes of surgery, the child's heart beat became erratic and his blood pressure bottomed out.

"Damn it," she muttered, shoving another sponge into the

small abdominal cavity. Her heart pounded painfully against her chest. Losing a patient was bad enough. Losing a child always took a piece of her soul.

"Do something, Guy. We're losing him."

"I am," the anesthesiologist answered from behind the drape. "You do your job, and I'll do mine," he snapped. "Call the night supervisor to get another two units of blood over here, STAT," he yelled at the circulating nurse.

Tess's vision momentarily blurred. Her stomach fell to her knees as she realized the odds were against her saving this child. Shoving her emotions back into their lockbox, she refocused on the task at hand, jerking out a soaked sponge and jabbing in another.

"Suction," she ordered.

The suction tube tip snaked into the cavity. Red fluid flowed through the clear tube and dumped into the receiver. Out of the corner of her eye, Tess saw the anesthesiologist hang yet another bag of blood. The bleeding in the child's abdomen continued unabated by anything she did.

Damn it! It looked like the fresh blood was racing straight from the bag into her surgical field. She lifted his stomach and found another small oozing tear.

"Suture," she said and, without pause, a threaded needle was slapped into her hand. The hole was tiny and stitched easily, but then her patient was tiny also. Even damage this slight was significant to a child of this weight and age.

"Blood pressure dropping," Guy said, his voice tight with tension. "Down to fifty over thirty. I'm increasing fluids, now."

The child's heart sputtered and stilled. The alarm on the heart monitor screamed. The sound echoed off the tile walls.

"Pushing epinephrine now," Guy said, his words clipped.

"Damn it." Tess began chest compressions. "Crash cart,"

she snapped at the circulator, who'd already begun rolling the four-drawer cart.

"Charge to 200," Tess directed.

Sue powered up the defibrillator and handed the paddles to Tess.

"Clear." Tess waited a couple of seconds for the surgery team to break contact with the patient before delivering the electrical shock to the heart. The heart monitor continued its prolonged squeal in the background.

"Charge to 300. Clear."

She delivered a second jolt and waited for the heart to beat. When the small heart continued to remain motionless, she restarted chest compressions.

"Pushing magnesium," Guy said, raising his voice to be heard above the loud drone of the heart monitor.

"Charge to 300 again," Tess said.

Sue handed her the paddles.

"Clear." Tess shot another electrical jolt to the heart.

No response. She restarted manual heart compressions. Blood gushed with each compression. She was losing him. She knew it. She didn't want to accept it, but deep down in her soul, a chunk broke off and lodged in her throat. It was impossible to swallow the lump when she had no saliva in her mouth.

"Don't leave us now," she coaxed through pursed lips. "Come on, baby. Come on."

For just a second, the child's heart thumped. The beat was slow and it was thready, but his tiny heart was beating on its own. Tess's own heart leaped in jubilation.

"Blood pressure forty over ten," Guy said, a hint of optimism coloring his words. Then, "Shit! Heart rate dropping. Blood pressure thirty-five over zero."

The tiny heart stopped again. Nothing Tess or Dr. Madison tried got it restarted. Twenty minutes of CPR left

Tess sweating. Every muscle in her body was so rigid it was painful, but the extended CPR couldn't get her patient's heart going. She'd lost him.

Tess drew in a deep breath, glanced at the wall clock, and then called it. "Time of death, two twenty-two a.m." Her voice choked on unspent tears. Now was not the time and it certainly wasn't the place.

"I never even saw his face," she said, her voice dropping.

The anesthesiologist unclipped the divider sheet and Tess got her first glimpse of her patient's face. She gasped. The muscles in her legs shook and threaten to collapse under her. She grasped the OR table for support. Oh, God. A sob caught in her throat.

She saw this face in her dreams almost every night.

Preston's son's looked so much like her son who'd died at birth.

———

Tess looked through the window into the surgery waiting room. Only two people occupied the area, so moving them to a private consultation area wouldn't be necessary.

The woman sagged over the arm of the waiting room sofa. Tears flowed steadily down her cheeks; long lines of black mascara streaked her pale face. Her blond hair, once in a stylish chignon, hung in lifeless strands around her shoulders. Her black—and obviously expensive—cocktail dress was wrinkled with dirt around the hem and on the skirt. The black stockings on her legs were torn with numerous runs. A pair of expensive Jimmy Choo shoes lay on the floor in front of her.

The man, with his dark hair and olive skin tones, stood wide-legged looking out a window into the darkness. His hands were clasped tightly behind his back. Like his wife, his clothes bore the rips and embedded dirt from the accident.

Tess's heart seized and she bit back her tears. She hated giving bad news. It was part of her job, without doubt the worst part. And as much as she hated the man in the waiting room—and she did despise him—and as awful as he and his wife felt now, Tess was getting ready to blow their world apart even more. She took no pleasure in that.

She glanced toward Sue, who had come from the OR with her. "God, I hate this."

Bringing the nurse from the OR with her was out of the ordinary, but given her history with her patient's father, she needed the support.

"You ready?"

Sue's lips pressed into a thin line and she nodded.

Tess took a deep breath and opened the door.

At the sound of the door opening, Preston Lloyd whirled around. His gaze met Tess's and the muscles in his face pulled as his jaw tightened. He walked over and sat by his wife

"Mr. Lloyd. Mrs. Lloyd," Tess began.

His eyes hardened as his glare hit her. She fought to maintain her professional attitude and tone.

Constance Lloyd looked at her, hope flashing in her eyes. Tess hated that look, especially knowing she would be delivering the worse news a mother could receive.

Tess pulled up a chair across from the couple and sat. "I'm Dr. Sweeney. I am so sorry but—"

"No!" Constance's scream reverberated off the walls. "No. No. No. No. No." She let out a loud wail of pain, and hit her husband's arm with her fist. "No. Not my baby. My baby." She socked his arm again before collapsing on the sofa cushions away from him.

Preston leaned forward, both hands resting on his knees like a cat ready to pounce.

Sue hurried over, sat on the arm of the sofa, and wrapped her arms around the hysterical mother, holding Constance Lloyd as her body shook in anguish. The woman's cries and shrieks echoed off the walls of the large waiting room.

Tess looked at Preston. "I am so sorry. When Hunter landed, his internal organs were jerked around violently. There were numerous tears in the blood vessels that fed the organs. There was just too much organ damage and too much blood loss. We did everything we could. I am sorry." She looked at Constance. "I am so sorry for your loss, Mrs. Lloyd," she said and glanced back at Preston.

He glared at her, black hate flaring in his eyes. "He was my son, my *only* son."

Her heart tore at his pain, even as her revulsion of being in the same room with him pressed her to leave. "I know, and I'm sorry. If I can do anything please let me know."

"I think you've done enough, Dr. Sweeney," he said with a sneer.

Tess didn't respond. Even if there were anything she could say or do to comfort him or his wife, he'd never accept it from her.

Their affair had been a flash fire, burning red-hot and leaving nothing behind when it was over, except distrust and hurt feelings. She'd been so young and naïve back then. Believed everything Preston had told her. Separated. Divorce filed. He couldn't live without her. Stupid to not have seen through his slick promises.

And tonight, nothing she could ever say would convince him she hadn't killed his child...not the one tonight or the one five years ago.

"I'm sorry," she said again and walked from the room into the hall. Her own grief ate at her gut like acid. Her heart ached for the parents and for herself. She stood for a minute trying to collect her emotions.

"Tess."

Her name was soft on Kyle's voice. She looked up and into his dove-colored eyes and found some of the strength she needed.

"Hey. I heard. I'm sorry, baby," he said.

A hand clasped down hard on her shoulder and wheeled her around. Preston Lloyd had followed her from the room and now glared at her, his jaw flexing and relaxing. "Excuse us, Sheriff. Tess and I need to have a private conversation," he said and jerked Tess off to one side.

"I want to know why you killed my son. Did you think it would be the perfect revenge? The perfect way to get back at me? Did you? Did you? It was just a car accident. There's no way my son could have died from it." His voice vibrated with rage. His hands were rolled into tight fists at his side.

"That's enough, Lloyd." Kyle said, stepping between them.

"You bitch." He leaned toward Tess, pointing his finger in her face. "I'll have your license, Tess. I'll personally see to it that you never kill another person."

"Preston, I—" Her heart thumped painfully against her chest. Diamond Lakes was a small town with a tight medical community. Preston had enough political clout to ruin her career if he so chose.

"I said that's enough." Kyle pressed his hand on Lloyd's chest to hold him away from Tess. All he was missing was the suit of armor.

She shouldn't be relieved to have Kyle protecting her. She should be strong enough to stand up for herself. But she was so tired, so heartbroken, so fragile right now. A single word could reduce her to tears. When she laid her hand on Kyle's back, the muscles were tense and strained.

Preston shoved Kyle's shoulder to dislodge his restraining hand. "You stay out of this, Monroe—if you want to keep your job as sheriff. I can make your reelection campaign fizzle before it starts." He glared at Tess over Kyle's shoulder. "This is between me and this lying, vindictive murderer. She killed my son."

Kyle placed his hand on Preston's shoulder and squeezed. Preston flinched. "That's more than enough. Dr. Sweeney isn't to blame. I'm sorry for your loss, Preston. You need to go see to your wife."

Preston jerked his shoulder out of Kyle's grasp. "This isn't over, Tess. Not by a long shot. I'll be contacting the head of hospital, the chairman of the board, and the president of the Texas Medical Society and filing a complaint about you with each of them. I promise you, I will find a way to ruin your life like you ruined mine tonight." He stormed away, slamming the surgery waiting room door against the wall.

———

PRESTON WALKED AWAY from the conniving bitch, his hands in tight fists to keep from wrapping them around her skinny, murderous neck. There was no reason for her to have taken the position of chief of surgery at St. Michael's except to be near him. She'd been a clingy girlfriend and he'd dumped her like the trash she was.

He still could hardly believe that she'd had the nerve to become pregnant with his child and lie to him about it. *To him!* He could recognize perjury when he heard it. That was one of his talents that made him such a good lawyer.

And that this bitch thought she could feed him a story about an abortion just so she could keep a part of him with her the rest of her life. Disgusting. God was on his side, as He should be. Even He had known she would be a horrible mother and He'd taken that fetus from her. The insane thing was that she blamed *him*, not God, where the blame should have been laid.

However, if this lying woman had had the gall to carry his baby to term after she'd told him she'd had an abortion, he'd have taken the kid away and put it with adoptive parents. Bringing a bastard child into his home would have been an insult to the sanctity of his marriage.

Plus, the voters would never have forgiven him.

The vindictive woman had probably dreamed of a night like this...a night when she could extract her revenge on him. He'd expected it, but he'd never imagined she was sick enough to kill his son...the *only* son he'd ever have.

As he made his way back to his wailing, stupid wife, he promised that Tess Sweeney would regret ever meeting him.

CHAPTER THREE

Kyle turned and placed both hands on Tess's shoulders. With a gentle tug, he eased her up to him. "Tess. I'm sorry. Preston didn't mean any of that. People say shit like that when they're upset. He had to lash out at someone. I'm just sorry it was you."

He massaged her neck and shoulders. Instead of his touch producing comfort, her muscles stiffened to the elasticity of concrete slabs.

"Don't," she said, and moved a couple of steps away. With a surreptitious glance she checked the area and was fairly certain their actions hadn't been observed. "I appreciate your concern, Kyle, but Preston reminds me of an injured wild animal. In pain and ready to strike out at someone. I'm pretty sure that will be me. I'd hate to see you go down as collateral damage."

She blew out a long breath in frustration. Everything medically possible had been done for Preston's son. She had no doubt that the OR staff would back her up. However, if Preston went ahead with his threats—and sadly, she knew him well enough to believe he would—her life would be a living hell. Negative publicity could kill her career, even if she were later found to be in the right. Patients wouldn't want to take a chance that she'd messed up in surgery and killed her patient.

And voters wouldn't reelect a sheriff who was known to be at odds with a popular prosecuting attorney, even if the sheriff's department wasn't responsible for the accident investigation.

Damn. She liked it here in Diamond Lakes. Great house. Great practice. A budding romance. And the worst mistake of her life—Preston Lloyd—had the potential power to take it all away.

The overhead call system clicked on. There was a second of brief static before the operator said, "Dr. Sweeney. Call extension four-six-seven. Dr. Sweeney. Call four-six-seven."

"Wonder why they didn't just call your cell," Kyle said.

"I don't know." She pulled her phone from her pocket. There were seven missed calls. "Damn, I forgot I put in on silent when I went in to talk with the Lloyds." She lifted the receiver off the house phone and dialed.

"Four West."

"Hi, this is Dr. Sweeney. I was paged to this extension."

"Hold on a sec, Dr. Sweeney." Tess heard clacking as the phone was passed to another person. "Dr. Sweeney. This is Becca Adams. I've got Freddy Worthington up here on four."

"Okay. What's the problem?"

"We have him up here just for overnight observation, but he's having trouble breathing and he's complaining of a sharp chest pain that wasn't there a while ago. The veins in his neck have become much more pronounced and he's a little cyanotic around his mouth. His heart rate is up to one-twenty. I'm wondering if maybe he's developed a pneumothorax."

"Good thought, Becca. Could also be pulmonary contusion. I'm headed your way." She looked at Kyle as she replaced the receiver. "Gotta go. Thanks for running interference for me."

"Sure. What's the problem?" he asked with a nod to the phone.

"Worthington kid is having problems."

She hurried down the hall to the stairwell instead of using the hospital elevators that were notoriously slow. Taking the stairs two at a time, she raced up the two flights quickly. She jerked the door to Four West open and dashed to the nurses' station. Becca Adams was waiting for her.

"I swear, Dr. Sweeney, his condition has gotten worse in the couple of minutes since we talked," Becca said as the two women headed down the hall to room forty-one-fourteen.

"Has he had a chest film yet?"

Becca shook her head. "There wasn't a reason to."

"You guys have a portable ultrasound on the floor?"

"No, but I can get one from labor and delivery pretty quick."

"Do that. Order a portable chest X-ray too. What about blood work?"

"Did the usual CBC with diff in the ER and a type and cross, but that's about it. I should mention Worthington is slurring his words. Seems kind of out of it. Confused. You know?"

"Did anyone draw a blood alcohol?"

"Don't think so. If they did, I haven't see it."

"Get a blood alcohol STAT. If we have to do surgery, we'll need to know that."

"Got it."

"On second thought, what about a blood glucose?"

The nurse shook her head. "Haven't seen one."

"I'm wondering... Lloyd said the kid was drunk, slurring his words, stumbling around, things like that. I'm surprised no one drew an alcohol level." Before Becca could respond, Tess added, "Of course his daddy is a judge so that might have played into that decision." Living in a small Southern community had opened her eyes to the political sway that elected officials had. She didn't like it, but then reality wasn't always how it was portrayed on television and movies.

"Probably," Becca agreed.

Tess pushed open the hospital room door. A large teenage boy lay on the bed, his eyes wide, the blue tinge to his skin pronounced. Someone had had the forethought to start him on oxygen. She checked the flow...six liters per minute. Fine for now.

On the far side of the bed, a heavy-set man—Judge Worthington, she assumed—and matching heavy-set women —Mrs. Worthington—stood. Parental concern etched worry lines on both their faces.

"I'm Dr. Sweeney," Tess said. "I hear our boy is having a little trouble."

"Frederick Worthington," the man said. "My wife, Helena. Freddy was doing pretty good until about half an hour ago. Said his chest and shoulders were hurting. I just thought it was from hitting the steering wheel."

"No air bag?"

"No. It was an old truck."

Tess pulled her stethoscope from her pocket while Becca entered the lab and radiology orders into the bedside computer. Tess placed the stethoscope bell on Freddy's chest. She moved it from one side to the other and then back again. There were no breath sounds on the left side of his chest. His heart was racing. The blue around his mouth was getting darker. She opened her mouth to tell Becca to get that chest study STAT when the door slammed open and the portable machine rolled into the room.

"Great. I need that X-ray STAT. Judge. Mrs. Worthington. Would you please step out in to the hall while we do this?"

"Oh, dear," Mrs. Worthington moaned. "I don't know." She wrung her hands.

"Come on, Mrs. W., Judge. I'll show you where you can wait," Becca said as she gently, but forcibly, lead them from the room.

Nice work, Tess thought.

"What's going on?" Freddy gasped from the bed. "I...I... can't breathe."

"Hang on, pal," Tess cooed. "Let's take a quick look."

The X-ray technician positioned the film cartridge behind Freddy's back and the machine's cone over his chest. Everyone stepped into the hall for the brief second it took to shoot the X-ray. Then the room was full again with the technician, the nurse, Tess and now the lab technician, who went quickly to the patient's side to get his blood sample.

"Ready," the X-ray tech said.

Tess studied the results on the X-ray monitor. What an advantage to be able to see the digital X-rays on the computer immediately rather than waiting for the slow film-developing process of the old days. As she studied the image, her heart rate ramped up. Damn. Worse than she'd thought. Looked like a pneumothorax-hemothorax combo. Kid couldn't get a break.

She grabbed the lab tech as he passed. "Add a CBC with diff to those orders. I need the results STAT and I mean STAT like in five minutes, not fifteen. Call the results to the OR. Got it?"

The young male technician—probably a recent graduate given his crummy shift schedule—nodded. "Yes, ma'am, er, doctor."

"Becca, call the OR. I need a room now. Tell them I've got

blood and air in the chest. I'll have to do a chest tube but I want to do it in an OR."

"On it," Becca said, moving rapidly to the room phone.

"You done with me?" the X-ray tech asked.

"Done. Thanks for being fast."

He nodded and rolled the machine into the hall.

"Got you a room," Becca announced as she hung up the phone.

"Grab the parents and a consent form."

Becca nodded and headed from the room.

The room cleared. In the quiet, Freddy's labored breathing sounded loud and harsh. His face reflected his anxiety and fear.

"Okay, Freddy. It's just me and you for a minute. I need to know something. Did you drink any beer, or wine, or anything tonight? Take any drugs? This is important. I have to know the truth."

He shook his head.

"I know you're scared," Tess said, taking his clammy hand. "I would be too if I didn't know what was going on. Your parents are on their way back, and I'll explain it to all of you, but I have to know about any drugs or alcohol. It's important. I'm taking you to surgery. You have blood and air in your chest. Do you understand?"

He nodded.

"Okay. If you had any booze or drugs tonight, I have to be able to tell the anesthesiologist. I'm not the cops. I'm not your parents. This doesn't have anything to do with getting into trouble. One more time, did you have anything to drink tonight? Take any drugs at all? Smoke a little pot? Anything?"

He shook his head vigorously.

"Has anyone ever suggested you had diabetes or a problem with your blood sugar?"

He shook his head.

Behind her, the door burst open and his parents rushed in, followed by Becca. In her hand Becca carried a clipboard with the OR consent form. Tess took the form and turned to Freddy's parents.

"Judge. Mrs. Worthington. I've explained this to Freddy. He broke a couple of ribs in the accident. One of those ribs has punctured his lung. He's got air in his chest, which I could treat easily enough, but I'm worried about the blood around his lungs. The air could be handled with a simple chest tube, as could the blood there. Usually this could be done outside an operating room, but I'd like to do the chest-tube insertion in the OR because of the volume of blood I'm seeing on the X-ray. This OR form gives me permission to do the chest tube and, if I feel it's necessary, to do exploratory surgery to see where the blood is coming from. I'll know more once I get him in the OR."

"Can't you just put in the tube and then if he's needs surgery, come ask us?" Mrs. Worthington asked in a trembling voice. Her face was a mask of alarm. Her eyes sparkled with unshed tears.

"Yes, I could, but we would lose a lot of critical time if the bleeding worsens."

Judge Worthington put his hand on his wife's arm. "Helena, the doctor knows what she's doing. Let her do her job." He looked at Tess, fear and concern pulling his mouth into a taut line. "Do what you need to. Give me the form. I'll sign."

Tess handed him the clipboard. "One more thing. I looked through the family history taken in the ER. Has anyone ever mentioned Freddy having trouble with his blood sugar?"

The Worthingtons exchanged glances. "No," Helena Worthington said. "But my mother had the sugar diabetes. Why? Are you telling me Freddy has it too?"

Tess shook her head. "No. I'm just following up on some of his symptoms." She took the form back and signed her name to the form before passing it to Becca to sign as a witness. "Y'all can wait in here during surgery. I'll let you know as soon as we know anything." To Becca, she said, "OR transport here yet?"

Becca nodded. "Yes, ma'am."

She opened the door and waved. Three scrub-clad women came into the room with a transport gurney. Grabbing his undersheet, they deftly moved him onto the gurney and out the door.

"I'll talk to you in a bit," Tess said and followed her patient to the OR suite.

After tying a mask around her nose and mouth, Tess put her protective glasses back on, and stepped up to the sink to do a scrubbing routine she'd done more times than she could count. As she scrubbed, she watched the staff transfer Freddy to the OR table. Dr. Guy Madison again stood at the head of the table ready to provide the anesthesia support she needed.

As the door to the room opened, she called in, "Hey, Guy. Glad to see you again."

"Let's try not to make these midnight visits a regular thing, okay?" Guy replied with a lift of his eyebrows.

"No kidding. He under yet?"

The anesthesiologist held up one finger. While Tess waited, she called over to the circulating nurse. "Nina. I need this patient's lab work. Can you check and see if we've got it? If not, tell the lab my foot is going to be up someone's ass. I need those results now."

"Yes, ma'am," Nina replied. She headed back to the nurses' station. Nina was back with a laboratory printout before Tess had finished scrubbing. "Here ya go." She held up the paper so Tess could read it.

"Thanks." Tess rinsed and, holding her hands up, backed

into the operating room. After accepting the sterile towel to dry her hands, she said, "Guy. Check these lab results. Look at his blood sugar. Report I had was the kid was drunk at the scene. Speech slurred. Stumbling around. Almost incoherent. But no alcohol in his blood. None at all."

Guy took the results and studied them. "What are you thinking? Some type of diabetic ketoacidosis?"

"Yep," Tess said as she slid her arms into the second surgical gown of the night. "I'm thinking he got D-five-W in the ambulance, and that helped his blood sugar. What you got running his line?" Nina pulled sterile gloves over Tess's hands.

"Ringers Lactate."

Tess nodded. "Good. Okay, ladies and gentlemen, let's go."

Unlike her first surgery of the night, this one couldn't have gone any smoother. The chest tube slid in like a toothpick through a drink straw. The blood flowing in the tube was dark. Definitely not fresh. She attached the chest tubing to the collection chamber, made sure everything was secure.

"If only every surgery went that easy," Tess said with a smile.

"I'd take it," Guy replied.

Tess stepped away from the table and ripped off her gown. "I'll head down and talk to the parents. I'll meet you all in the recovery room."

She found the Worthingtons where she'd left them. Their heads snapped up when she stepped into the room.

"All good news," she said.

Helena Worthington burst into tears. Her husband hugged her. Tess could see him fighting back his own tears.

"Got the tube in with no problems at all. The bleeding is stopped and I'm not expecting it to begin again. Freddy's in recovery now."

"Can we see him?" Helena asked.

"Not right now. He'll be back in here soon. He'll have a tube coming out his chest about right here." Tess pointed to her right side under her arm. "It'll be connected to a box that'll be hanging on his bed. You'll see bubbles in the fluid inside that box. That's normal."

"Thank you, Doctor Sweeney," Judge Worthington said.

Tess nodded, relieved to be giving good news this time. Inside her soul, where she'd been gloomy, the smiling faces of the Worthingtons brought light to all those dark places, chasing away her shadows.

"Who is Freddy's regular doctor? I'm a little concerned about his blood sugar."

"He sees Dr. Owens," Mrs. Worthington answered.

Tess went on to explain about low blood sugar and how it can make people appear drunk when they weren't.

"I've heard about that," the judge said. "Had one guy claim that in my court once. I thought it was just bull."

"No, it's very real, judge. I know Dr. Owens. I'll make sure the nursing staff knows to contact him."

Freddy's mother stood and hugged Tess. "I don't know how to thank you."

Tess smiled. "I'm glad I was in the hospital." To both the Worthingtons, she said, "You two need to get some rest. You've done everything for Freddy you can tonight. Go home and get some sleep. That's what he's going to be doing for a while."

"Oh, no," Helena Worthington said. "I couldn't possibly leave." She looked at her husband. "You should get some sleep, Frederick. I'll stay here tonight."

Tess's heart ached as she saw and heard the love Helena Worthington had for her family. She envied the woman. The odds were stacked against Tess ever having another baby, and that made her sad. It also drove away most men her age. They all wanted children—their own blood children. Adoption was usually out of the question...or at least that was true of the men she'd dated.

Now was neither the time nor the place for these feelings, so Tess locked them away until she could express them, preferably in private, alone, and in the dark.

The powerful judge took her hand. "Thank you, Dr. Sweeney. We are in your debt."

She hurried away. The back of her throat ached. The back of her eyes burned with unshed tears. Privacy. She had to find a place and soon. A surgeon never cried in public...never ever.

On the surgery schedule board, she left a note for the morning OR crew to find her in a call room and wake her at six. On the fourth floor, she found an empty call room. She let herself in and locked the door behind her. Falling on the bed face first, she at last let all her suppressed tears flow, soaking the bed linens.

It seemed like the minute she'd finally turned off her brain and dropped off, someone was pounding on her door.

"Dr. Sweeney?"

Tess groaned and pulled her wrist closer to her face, trying in vain to read the numbers on her watch. "What?" Her voice cracked with the word.

"It's Tia Brown, from the OR. There's a note on the board to find you and wake you up at six."

Tess groaned again. She'd forgotten she'd left a wake-up-call note. "Okay. Thanks."

Six! How could it be six? She'd just shut her eyes. She stood, stretched sore muscles, and pasted a smile on her face. Slapping her emotions back into their secure lockbox, she headed for her first surgical case of the day.

She did four cases, made hospital rounds—taking extra time to check on Freddy, who was doing great—and finished the day seeing post-surgical patients in her office. As awful as her day had began losing the Lloyd child in surgery, the rest of day progressed smoothly. Her surgeries went off without a hitch. Her hospital patients were up and mobile. Her office patients were healing well and most were quite pleased with their progress. So why did she feel the sword of Damocles hanging over her head?

CHAPTER FOUR

About four p.m., the sword finally fell in the form of a telephone call from Dr. Troy Monroe's secretary. Dr. Monroe wanted to meet with her as soon as possible.

Damn Preston Lloyd. Had he really filed a complaint with the hospital?

At five p.m., she walked into the hospital chief of staff's office, her heart doing a tachycardic tango with her lungs. Forcing a calm expression on her face—one that did not come close to matching her jumping insides—she tapped on Dr. Monroe's office door.

"Come in."

Troy Monroe was Sheriff Kyle Monroe's identical twin. And even though she'd never been in the same room with the Monroe brothers at the same time, she'd bet she'd know which one was Kyle. However, it still jarred her senses to see a likeness of the man who'd been naked in her bed last night now sitting behind a large and, her opinion, intentionally intimidating desk. Probably overcompensating for an inadequate male package...not that Kyle had that problem. But this guy...

"Good afternoon, Dr. Sweeney." Troy Monroe stood and gestured to a seat in front of his desk. "Please sit," he said, retaking his massive leather chair—over compensating again —and putting his desk between them.

Tess took a seat as directed. She waited for Monroe to make the first move. When he didn't say anything, or at least didn't speak quickly enough for her, she said, "You called this meeting. What's on your mind?"

Troy Monroe leaned back in his chair, apparently unaccustomed to doctors not being awed in his presence, or maybe he was accustomed to women being cowed in his office. He hadn't been chief of staff when Tess had been hired as chief of surgery, but she'd heard rumors that he'd spoken against her hiring to the board.

The board had hired her anyway.

That had been two years ago. She still didn't know if he felt she was unqualified for the job, or didn't like a female in a position of authority, or if he'd had another candidate in mind for her job. Regardless, the nurses had clued her in that when Monroe had become chief last year, her surgeries had begun being covertly monitored, but not so clandestine as to keep it off the hospital staff grapevine...a powerful source of information.

Monroe steepled his fingers. "I had a visit from a very distraught parent today."

She said nothing.

"I'm assuming you know to whom I'm referring."

Tess leaned back in her chair, crossed her legs, and mimicked his steepled fingers. She swallowed and forced a calm expression on her face. "Tell me more."

The chief's face set into a harsh mask. He leaned toward her. His eyes took on a hard glare. "Preston Lloyd was in my office this afternoon. He tells me your inadequate surgical skills failed to save his child after a simple, non-fatal accident." The muscles in Monroe's cheeks flexed. "Additionally, he said you were impaired."

"Impaired?" Tess's eyebrows shot up. "Impaired, as in exactly what?"

"As in you'd been drinking."

Tess's hand slapped the arms of the chairs. "That is a lie."

"Which part? Your surgical inadequacies or your drunkenness?"

"All of it. Preston Lloyd is full of crap. His son died on the OR table, but we did everything we could do to save him. The damage to all his internal organs was just too much. The child was small for his age and his blood loss was massive. I'm sure Guy Madison would be happy to tell you about our efforts to save the Lloyd child."

Anger rolled through her. Hot flashes of fury seared her blood. That bastard Lloyd thought he could take her down? Well he had another thing coming.

"And exactly how much had you had to drink last night, Dr. Sweeney?"

"Not a drop."

Troy Monroe shrugged. "I guess we'll never know if you're telling the whole story or not since any alcohol in your system has long since been metabolized. But you had a problem a few years ago, isn't that right?"

She decided to ignore that dig into her past. She'd been honest with the board about her history when she was hired. Monroe had to have read her personnel record and already knew the answer to his question. The jerk was just trying to unnerve her. It wasn't going to work.

"Want to know why Preston Lloyd wasn't in your office first thing this morning instead of this afternoon?" She held up her hand when Monroe opened his mouth to respond. "It doesn't matter what he told you about why he waited until late in the afternoon to call. The reason was he was drunk as a skunk last night. He couldn't show up here still intoxicated. He had to go home and get all the booze out of his system."

This time, it was Monroe who lifted an eyebrow. "And you know this because you drew a blood alcohol? No, wait. No blood was drawn." He snapped his fingers. "I know. The state troopers at the scene did a breathalyzer and it registered greater than a zero point eight?" He knitted his brows as though confused. "No, that's not it. So exactly how did you, without any tests, determine our esteemed prosecuting attorney was *drunk as a skunk* I think you said?"

Her blood boiled with rage. "I have a nose," she said, jabbing her finger against her right nostril. "I could smell the bourbon."

"I bet you could," he said with a smirk. He leaned back in his chair. "Whether Mr. Lloyd was inebriated isn't at issue. At issue is your performance and whether you were impaired."

Tess was not going to let this self-righteous prick run her off from a job and town she loved. As she had that thought, she wasn't sure if the prick in question was Monroe or Lloyd...or hell, maybe both.

She stood. "My surgical skills are outstanding. Lloyd's child had a bad outcome that had nothing to do with my performance. Everything that could have been done was done. As far as booze goes, I do not drink. Ever." She picked up her briefcase from the floor. "If you are planning a formal investigation, please let me know now so that I can hire legal representation. If you just are going to nose around in my cases as you've been doing over the past six months, feel free. I have nothing to hide. Now, if you'll excuse me, I've had a long day."

She moved to leave.

"Dr. Sweeney." His voice was like iron.

She turned back but said nothing.

"At this time, I'll not initiate a formal inquiry. However, I will be talking with the staff involved in the case as well as asking for the child's autopsy to be done STAT."

She shrugged. "It's your time to waste."

"Yes, it is."

Closing the door behind her, it was all she could do not to slam it, open it, and slam it again. The arrogant prick. To think that he and Kyle had shared a uterus, parents, and similar upbringing scrambled her mind. It completely defied understanding that Kyle could be so strong and so caring while his twin brother was a condescending, self-important jackass.

She sighed and made her way to her car. If only she could have just one drink. Her mind sent the taste of cold vodka sliding down her throat. Just one drink and the pain would go away. She'd forget her son's face. She'd forget the day Preston had ordered her to get an abortion. She'd forget today totally.

But one drink always led to another and another and another, until there was nothing left in the bottle. She'd tried losing herself in a bottle once. It hadn't worked then, so why would it work now?

Because now she was an adult...a different person. A person capable of controlling her impulses. A person with the ability to have a single drink and then set the bottle down.

The short drive home took her past restaurants, grocery stories, drug stores, and two package liquor stores. Ten different places in a ten-minute drive to get a drink or a bottle of vodka.

Damn it. She was a doctor. There wasn't anything she couldn't do. Besides, who would know? A short stop would take care of her day nicely.

She pulled into her garage, cut the engine, lowered the door, and just sat there, too depleted emotionally and physically to move. Today had been the day from hell. Dropping her head forward to rest on the steering wheel, she sighed. Her shoulders sagged under the weight of all her stress.

Between surgeries, hospital rounds, and office visits, she hadn't allowed herself to think about the early morning surgery. Could she have done anything different? Better?

And poor Kyle, just dating her would suck him into a vortex of her problems. She didn't have ESP nor fortune-telling skills inherited from a long-dead relative, but deep in her gut, she knew a continued relationship with her would threaten Kyle's career and his bond with his brother. And while she and Dr. Monroe did not like each other much, Kyle loved his brother. He was too good of a man to lose that connection all because of her.

And Preston, damn his soul to hell. Their affair had been hot enough to challenge the sun for dominance. There'd been an unquenchable desire that'd burned like an inferno...until the woman he was divorcing had called to tell him she was pregnant. Talk about a man singing a different song after that.

She pulled herself out of her car and shuffled into her kitchen, carrying the fifth of vodka from the last liquor store before she reached home. Setting it on the counter, she stared at it for a long time before turning her gaze out her bay window toward Happy Jack Lake. A long sigh slid from her lungs. The water. That's exactly what she needed. Her boat. She could usually find the solitude she needed on the water.

After changing clothes and pouring the entire tray of ice from her freezer into a cooler, she shoved the vodka on top, grabbed the keys to her boats and headed out.

———

PRESTON LLOYD DRANK SO much coffee between three a.m. and noon, he was pretty sure his green eyes had to be brown.

But he had to be sharp this afternoon. He had to be his best. He had an appointment with Dr. Troy Monroe, Chief of Staff of St. Michael's Hospital, something he wasn't looking forward to. He didn't like Troy Monroe. The man was conceited. Thought the words doctor and God were interchangeable.

Monroe had been hired by the hospital board after an outbreak of Methicillin-resistant *Staphylococcus aureus*, aka MRSA, had caused the death of six hospitalized patients. The public outcry had been damaging to the hospital reputation, not to mention the financial bottom line. The hospital couldn't afford another public disaster, like an alcoholic doctor on staff.

But Preston didn't go into any courtroom underprepared. Before he met with Monroe, he had a long telephone conversation with his new friend, Roy McCall, the chairman of the hospital board of directors. McCall had been instrumental in Monroe's hiring, as well as Tess Sweeney's. Too bad Preston hadn't been able to stop Tess's hiring but he hadn't had McCall's ear back then. Now, however, a few choice words in McCall's ear, and he was ready to take whatever action needed to protect *his* hospital, as he called it. By the time Preston walked into Monroe's office for their meeting, he had all his guns loaded with facts, dates, and alcoholic incidents for Tess Sweeney.

That bitch would pay.

CHAPTER FIVE

"I want that Lloyd accident report on my desk today," Sheriff Kyle Monroe said as he walked through the Diamond Lakes County Sheriff Department bullpen.

"Yes, sir, Sheriff," the fresh-faced Adams replied. "I'm almost done."

Kyle rubbed his exhausted eyes and headed for the coffee pot. At this time of the day, the pot had been brewing a good twelve hours since the morning shift had arrived at five. The cup of joe was thick, black, and jarringly strong...just how he liked it. He carried his favorite mug—the one with a gun grip for the handle—back to his desk and dropped like a rock into his chair.

Damn, he was tired. Tucking his chin toward his chest, he rolled his head back and forth, the muscles in his neck making a grinding sound as though filled with sand. After a couple of neck rotations, his neck popped...not that it helped his stiff neck or mood. But at least he felt like he'd accomplished something, which was more than he could say for most of his time today.

"Sheriff?"

Kyle looked up. "What?"

"Here's our report from the Lloyd accident." Joseph Adams, the young deputy who'd helped secure the accident scene, set the paper report on Kyle desk.

Even though the accident wasn't his to investigate, preparing a written report would be a good learning experience for the deputy.

"In a nutshell, what happened?"

The deputy sighed. "We've got two different versions of the accident. The Worthington kid said the Lloyd car swerved into his lane and then back, but he couldn't react fast enough to avoid hitting the rear passenger door of the Lloyds' Lexus.

"Lloyd says the truck driven by Worthington swerved into his lane and hit him. Both drivers deny using alcohol or drugs, but the Worthington boy was slurring his speech pretty bad. He had a little trouble walking, but he blamed it on hitting his knees during the accident. Lloyd smelled heavily of alcohol, but he didn't appear too drunk."

"And what about the field breathalyzer?"

Adam's baby-fresh face reddened. "Sir. Lloyd told us that his wife had been holding a bottle of bourbon that broke during the impact and that's why he smelled like booze. Lloyd reminded us that he was the county prosecuting attorney and he would never drive if he'd been drinking. He didn't seem drunk and he needed to leave to be with his son at the hospital."

"And did you find a broken bottle at the scene?"

"Yes, sir."

Kyle leaned back in his chair. "Kid, you're new here, so let me tell you a little fact. The county DA doesn't have the authority to do anything to you if you are doing your job. In my opinion, field sobriety tests should have been done but..." He shrugged. "The state's in charge, and if they didn't do one, not a lot you can do. What about..." He looked at the report in his hand. "What about Frederick Worthington? Did you do field sobriety tests on him?"

"Yes, sir. No alcohol registered on the breathalyzer, but he was unsteady on his feet. Maybe he'd taken some other type of drug. We don't know."

"Tell me about the Lloyd child."

The deputy's eyes shifted from side to side as he tugged at the collar of his shirt. "Well, sir, Mr. Lloyd claims he and his wife had just picked up their son from the babysitter and were on their way home. He says the boy was secured in a child booster seat. However, when the Worthington truck hit the Lloyd's car, the child was thrown from the car. Mr. Lloyd claims his son was ejected from the booster seat, but we didn't find the seat. Mr. Lloyd stated he thought the booster seat had floated away in Ten Mile River." The deputy shrugged. "Could happen, I guess. The accident was right at the river's edge, and the water was flowing pretty hard and fast that night from all the rain we've had."

"I want to see that booster seat."

"We looked, sir."

"I want Ten Mile checked inch by inch. If that booster seat is there, I want it."

"Yes, sir."

"I'll contact Sheriff Singer's office. Ten Mile runs right through Whispering Springs. Maybe he can get his deputies to check the river down there for the missing child seat. Let me know if you have any other information about this."

"Will do, sir."

"So, who's telling the truth here?"

"My money is on Worthington, sir."

"And you figured this out how?" During their conversation, Kyle had been scanning the report. With the exception of not doing a breathalyzer on Lloyd, the deputy and his partner had done a thorough job with their investigation. But he didn't want to miss an opportunity to teach his deputy.

"Well, sir, I photographed and diagrammed the scene. I measured sixty feet of skid marks matching the tires of Mr. Worthington's Ford Bronco in the northbound lane. Based on skid-mark measurement and road conditions, I estimated Mr. Worthington's speed at thirty-six miles per hour.

"I measured tire marks moving from the northbound lane into the southbound and skid marks of seventy-five feet. These marks appear to be from the Lexus driven by Mr. Lloyd. Based on skid-mark measurements and road conditions, I estimated Mr. Lloyd's speed at fifty-four miles per hour."

Kyle nodded. "Good job. Hold on while I read your final paragraph." He adjusted the lamp on his desk to throw more light on the paper and read...

BASED UPON THE FACTS THAT ARE KNOWN TO ME AT THIS TIME, I AM OF THE OPINION THAT THE EVIDENCE DOES SUPPORT EITHER CRIMINAL CHARGES OR TRAFFIC INFRACTION VIOLATIONS. IN THIS CASE, A MINOR CHILD PASSENGER WAS EJECTED AS THE RESULT OF THE IMPACT AND LATER DIED. NO BOOSTER SEAT WAS LOCATED AT THE SCENE, AND NONE HAS BEEN LOCATED AT THE TIME OF THIS REPORT. NEITHER PARTY ADMITS TO EXCESSIVE SPEED, OR RECKLESS OR IMPROPER DRIVING. HOWEVER, I AM OF THE OPINION THAT BASED ON THE ONSITE SKID-MARK ANALYSIS, SPEED WAS A FACTOR IN THIS CASE. ADDITIONALLY, I AM OF THE OPINION THAT MR. LLOYD CROSSED THE CENTER LANE, PRECIPITATING THE ACCIDENT. SKID MARKS AT THE SCENE WOULD APPEAR TO SUPPORT THIS OPINION.

"So you think Lloyd was at fault?"

"Yes, sir."

"Good report. You can go, Adams. We'll talk later."

The twenty-something deputy turned to leave, then spun back. "Sir? I want it on the record that I think Lloyd was at fault and that our report will support filing charges."

"Thank you, Adams."

Kyle slid the unofficial report into the center drawer of his desk and locked it. He might never need this information, but if he did, he'd have it.

Damned shame for the Lloyds to lose their son. He hoped the state police had a report similar to the one his deputy had prepared. Lloyd might have to deal with a special prosecuting attorney, not to mention a seriously angry and hysterical wife.

He glanced at the clock and arched, stretching his cramped back muscles. It'd been a long day that'd started too early. Six deep gongs rang from the cuckoo clock his receptionist had given him last Christmas. Six p.m.

He'd called Tess a couple of times during the day, but she'd been either in surgery or unavailable for his calls. That wasn't like her, but he wasn't overly troubled. He knew her day had been as long and demanding as his.

He flipped open his cell and pressed the star key and one, the quick call number he'd assigned to Tess. Her phone rang a couple of times before voice mail picked up. He hung up, not leaving another message.

Not being able to talk to her today meant he'd been unable to assure her that Lloyd's angry rant had been just that, all rant and hot air. She didn't know that Preston was more at fault for his son's death than she'd ever be.

An ache in his gut had eaten at him all day. He should have tried harder this morning to reach her, reassure her, be there for her. Their relationship was new and fragile, easily destroyed by words said, or words not said.

Needing to see her, to hold her, he headed to her house.

He pulled into her drive and parked. A light from her kitchen window drew arcs on the concrete. Good. She was home. He rang the bell and waited. After of a couple of minutes of hearing no movement inside, he rang again.

"She not there," a tiny voice said.

He wheeled around and dropped his glance. A little blond-headed girl stood there, her thumb plugged snuggly in her mouth. He squatted.

"Hello there, Mattie. Does your mommy know where you are?"

About that time, he heard a frantic voice shouting, "Mattie. Mattie. Where are you?"

"Over here, Connie," he answered, picking up the little girl and holding her close to his chest.

Connie Blass had moved next door to Tess six months ago. She'd been a single parent with an infant after her husband had been killed in Iraq. He and Tess had babysat Mattie a number of times, both of them taking genuine pleasure in spoiling her rotten. He looked forward to the day he and Tess had their own child to spoil. Boy or girl didn't matter to him. Tess was wonderful with Mattie. She would make the best mother to as many children as he could talk her into having.

Connie's round face popped around a bush. "Thank God. I swear, I turn my back for one second..." She hurried across the lawn. "How many times do I have to tell you not to leave our driveway?"

Mattie wrapped her arms around Kyle's neck. "Mr. Kyle's here."

"I can see that," Connie said. "But that's no excuse for not minding."

The little girl squeezed tighter and buried her face into his neck. "I love Mr. Kyle."

Kyle's heart swelled inside his chest to the point he could hardly breathe. "I love you too, Mattie, but you have to do what your mother tells you to." He kissed her cheek and handed her over to Connie. "Here ya go."

Connie hugged her daughter before lightly patting her behind. "You scared me, pumpkin."

Kyle glanced toward Tess's door, which remained closed. "Hey, Connie. You see Tess today?"

Connie nodded. "Yeah. About thirty minutes ago. She flew out of here on that boat of hers like the devil himself was chasing her." She grinned. "I swear the woman has lake water in her veins instead of blood."

Kyle nodded. Of course. He should have thought about that. Connie's description was spot-on accurate.

"Thanks." He patted Mattie's back. "You be a good girl."

Kyle returned to his car wondering where Tess would be on Happy Jack Lake. He knew most of her favorite coves and hiding spots. Would it be a mistake to follow her? Did she really want to be alone? After all, he had left a number of messages today that she hadn't returned.

On the other hand, given how her morning had started, she might want a shoulder to lean on but was too stubborn to ask him for it. He drummed his fingers on the steering wheel for a couple of minutes before making up his mind.

Kyle tapped his phone on his thigh. He had to find Tess and talk to her. He scrolled through his stored directory until he found the listing he needed, pressed Send and waited for someone on the other end to answer.

"Deputy Barr," a deep voice said.

"Mark? Kyle Monroe here."

"Hey, Sheriff."

"You on lake patrol right now?"

"Yes, sir. What can I do for you?"

"I need a lift somewhere. Can you pick me up?"

"Somewhere, like on the lake?"

"Yup."

"No problem. Where are you now?"

"You know where Dr. Tess Sweeney's house is located?"

"Sure do."

"Sounds like you've been by there before."

Deputy Barr laughed. "Once or twice. Asked the lady out once. Got shot down big time." He sighed loudly. "Anyway, yeah. I know her place. You need me to pick you up there?"

"Yup."

"Be there in about ten."

"Works for me. I'll be on her dock."

Kyle slipped his phone back into its belt holder. He stepped from his sedan, locked the doors, then headed through Tess's gate into her yard. He'd first met Tess right here in her backyard, only then, it'd been overgrown with knee-high grass and rose bushes that'd been left to fend for themselves. Tess had reported a break-in and Kyle had responded since he was close.

It'd been hate at first sight. Tonight as he walked along a well-edged flagstone path marked by solar lighting with the scent of blooming roses in the air, he chuckled at the memory.

He'd called her a ball-busting bitch. She'd called him a straw-chewing, red-necked, backwoods Barney Fife. Their paths had continued to cross over the next two years, their public opinions never changing until Kyle had been shot six months ago and Tess had done the surgery that saved his life. When he'd awakened in recovery, Tess had been there. And again when he'd awakened in his room. He'd asked her out repeatedly for months, but she'd refused to see him socially until he was fully cleared as her patient.

They'd only been seeing each other for a couple of months. He hadn't expected his feelings for Tess to grow so deeply so quickly. It filled him with a mixture of terror and delight.

Kyle walked onto Tess's dock and sat in the cedar swing to wait. His cell phone's sharp shrill interrupted his thoughts, the sound echoing across the still water as though a multitude of phones had all gone off at one time. He pulled it off the belt holder expecting it to be Tess returning one of his many calls, but the readout said it was Troy Monroe.

"Hey, guy. What's going on?"

"It's been a bitch of day," his brother replied. "How about meeting me at the Water's Edge for some drinks and bro time?"

The Water's Edge was the current hot spot to drink and be seen, someplace he and Tess had been avoiding.

"Can't right now. What happened?"

Troy blew out a long breath. "I'm assuming you're on top of the Lloyd debacle from this morning?"

"I'm aware of it. The state police is handling the investigation. Why?" Kyle held his breath, hoping that sonofabitch Lloyd hadn't followed through with his ridiculous accusations against Tess.

"Lloyd was in my office this afternoon, steaming mad. Throwing around words like malpractice and lawsuit. Really went after Dr. Sweeney. You know her, right?"

Kyle forced himself to remain calm. Bastard Lloyd. "You know I know her. She did my surgery six months ago."

"Right, right. Well, Lloyd claims she was operating under the influence this morning. Said he could smell the alcohol on her breath after the surgery when she came to talk to him and his wife. Said Sweeney holds a personal grudge against him and his wife, and they didn't think she'd done all she could for his son."

"Really? Said all that, huh?"

"You know I've had my reservations about her as chief of surgery. She's been a pain in my ass since day one. Always wanting new and better equipment for the operating suites. Wanting additional nursing staff. Wanting more money for the staff. Always thinking she knows the best thing to do about everything. I'm thinking my gut was right and the board should have gone with Dr. Cartwright from California. Damn it."

Kyle could hear his brother taking another drink. Must have started without him.

"Lloyd can really make a shitstorm for the hospital, and frankly, for me too. He's already pulled Roy McCall in on the situation, and of course McCall is having one of his spastic fits about the hospital's reputation. McCall wants the situation resolved, like yesterday."

"Have you talked with Tess—Dr. Sweeney?"

"This afternoon after Lloyd left. She denied everything, of course. Fuck her, Kyle. She's gone. You know the board hired me to repair the hospital's reputation. We can't take any more bad press. Lloyd can make my life a living hel,l and I don't need it, especially over a doctor I didn't hire and already have reservations about."

As much as Kyle wanted to defend Tess, especially on the operating-while-under-the-influence-of-alcohol charge, he couldn't without violating her trust.

"Look, Troy. I think you need to hold off doing anything until the coroner has finished his autopsy and the accident's final report is done. In my opinion, Lloyd is full of bullshit. He's covering his own ass. My officers at the scene said he appeared fine but there was an alcohol smell on him and in his car. He claimed the smell was from a bottle of booze his wife was carrying home that broke when the accident occurred. Personally, I think that's crap."

"Doesn't matter. There has to be an informal in-house

inquiry into Dr. Sweeney's performance and conduct. If anything is found, we'll instigate a formal investigation."

"Dude. You'll ruin her career if you start digging around and implying she did something wrong."

"Can't be helped. Even if she didn't intentionally kill Lloyd's kid on the table, operating while drunk is a major problem."

"Did you ask her if she had a witness that could verify she hadn't been drinking?"

"She denies drinking but she didn't offer up any proof beyond her word."

Kyle had to bite his tongue from proclaiming her innocence in loud, unequivocal denials. *She wasn't drunk. She doesn't drink. Lloyd's actions contributed to his son's death, not Tess's surgical techniques.* To know all these personal tidbits, he'd have to go public with their relationship, something Tess had asked him not to do.

She did not want their relationship to be fuel for the hospital gossip mill. First, because Kyle had been her patient and she felt she skirted the line dating a former patient, even though their doctor-patient relationship had ended by the first date. And second, she didn't want the hospital staff or the chief of staff to think she was seeing the chief of staff's brother as a way to garner favored-nation status when it came to surgery schedules or the department getting its fair share of financial resources.

As she'd told him, her private life was her business. If Kyle wanted to be with her, he had to respect that. He was damned if he said anything and damned if he didn't.

However, Kyle knew Tess had been dead-cold sober when she'd done the surgery. In the month they'd been together, he'd never seen her take so much as a sip of alcohol. She'd passed it off as not liking the taste. He hadn't believed her but he hadn't challenged her on it either. When she was ready, she'd tell him everything.

His brother's in-house inquiry, no matter how limited, might reveal aspects about Tess she wasn't ready to discuss. He had to warn her.

"Bro? You still there?"

Kyle retuned back into the conversation. "I'm here. Just thinking."

"Sure you can't meet me for a drink or two? I'm buying?"

"You should buy. You have more money than sense." Troy laughed, but Kyle meant what he'd just said. If his brother had any sense about him, he'd realize backing Lloyd would be backing the wrong horse. "But not tonight. I've got some business I need to attend to."

"Okay, your loss. The Water's Edge is crammed with hot women tonight."

Troy had never been the same after finding his wife in bed with his best friend. It was as if he'd shut the door to anything that might convey a weakness, and that included any type of relationship. That'd been back when they'd been twenty-four. Kyle had been unattached and loved that his brother was back in the bars with him working the ladies. As identical twins, they got a lot of notice.

But Kyle had outgrown that scene. The only scene he wanted was the one that held only him and Tess Sweeney.

"Listen, Troy. I know you don't usually take my advice—"

"Damn straight. I'm the oldest, therefore the wisest," Troy said.

"Fine. I'm younger by two minutes, but listen to what I'm saying. Don't stake your career and reputation on Lloyd's word. It won't be a good move, bro."

"I don't know what bug you have up your ass about our prosecuting attorney, but the hospital board thinks he's wonderful. Between a lawyer with influence like Lloyd and a surgeon with an alcoholic history, I'll take the lawyer."

Kyle felt like he'd been gut shot. Tess had never mentioned being an alcoholic. Of course, that would make sense given her total abstinence. Still, she should have trusted him with this information.

"What do you mean a surgeon with an alcoholic history? Are you talking about Dr. Sweeney?"

"Damn straight. Lloyd clued me in on that little fact today. If I'd had known that back when you were shot, there's no way I'd have let her touch you."

Without being shot, Kyle doubted he'd have ever gotten to know Tess. Without getting to know her, he'd never have fallen so deeply in love with her. If his brother had known Tess's history, Kyle's life would be empty now, no Tess and her sparkling eyes. He thanked God Troy hadn't known.

The roar of an approaching boat drew Kyle's eye up the bay. The blue lights on the boat were whirling.

"I've got to run, Troy. Remember what I said."

CHAPTER SIX

Lloyd lifted the fifty-year-old scotch to his mouth, enjoying both the aroma of Scottish smoky peat and the smooth taste as the amber liquid filled his mouth. He'd inherited the scotch from his father. The bastard hadn't ever even opened the bottle. Only a fool would let liquor as fine as an Ardbeg Islay 1990 remain unopened. A scotch of this quality deserved to be drunk. Of course, his father hadn't had the refined taste buds that Preston had. Unlike his father, Preston could appreciate the subtleties of this excellent scotch.

He took his seat behind a massive stone desk in his private home office. As promised, he'd faxed a letter to the president of the Texas Medical Board requesting an inquiry into Dr. Tess Sweeney's actions the night Hunter died. He really should have found a way to stop the hospital from hiring her in the first place.

Damn board chairman McCall, his wife, and her equal-opportunity crap.

Tess's hiring had been a done deal before Preston had known about it, which was too bad. He probably could have put a stop to it, and then his son would still be alive.

He couldn't decide if McCall was smarter than he gave him credit for or stupid beyond words. Had McCall known that Tess and he had a past? When McCall had directed the board to hire Tess, had he done that to put a wedge between Preston and McCall's wife, with whom Preston had been having an affair for the past seven months? Or was McCall so ignorant as to hire a totally incompetent surgeon.

At this point, it didn't really matter, did it?

His jaw flexed as he ground his teeth. He'd had such high expectations for his son. Governor, or maybe senator. The boy had been sharp, just like his dad. God knew he hadn't taken after his mother, and for that, Preston had been thankful.

The thought of his spineless wife made his mouth curl into a snarl. He'd believed he was getting a skilled helpmate, someone with the right political and social connections he needed. Instead, he'd gotten a spoiled, weak whiner. She couldn't do anything right, from planning an appropriate reception to something as simple as picking out the right Christmas gifts for colleagues.

He tossed back the drink and refilled his glass.

Nothing but a bunch of worthless losers around him.

As soon as he'd dealt with Dr. Tess Sweeney, he'd deal with his whiny, pathetic wife. She was of no use to him now. Barren and socially inept, she'd become a hindrance for the future that awaited him.

He poured another splash of the expensive bottle of scotch before he stashed it behind a row of books. Constance would never appreciate it. No reason to let her find it.

Getting rid of Tess didn't mean she had to die. In fact, he'd rather she spent the rest of her pitiful behind bars.

And then there was Candy McCall, the hospital board chairman's wife. She'd become a problem of late. Candy had been good for a fast fuck, but as his next wife? Not hardly. She had to be almost thirty-nine.

No, he'd already looked through the possible replacements and found the perfect woman. Smart. Politically savvy. Socially connected. Belonged to the right political party. The daughter of a well-known state senator. Maybe a little young, but he believed in getting them young and training them right.

He knew what this state needed, and he knew he was the right man for the job. With his intelligence, good looks, and the right woman behind him, nothing could stop him from sweeping easily into the governorship of Texas. He just needed to clean up a little around him.

After tossing the liquid down his throat, he stood to head for bed. Tomorrow would require him to be with his wife all day, picking out a casket, and whatever else people had to do to bury someone. Constance had done all the planning when his father had died, so she'd know what to do...if he could keep her focused. Really, he should carry a small flask in his pocket tomorrow. Just enough to make the day tolerable.

CHAPTER SEVEN

Tess sucked on an ice cube, the melted cold liquid trickling down her throat. When the conversation with Troy Monroe cycled through her memory, she chomped down hard, shattering the cube into tiny slivers that melted rapidly on her tongue. Her right arm flopped over far enough to snag another chunk of ice. Instead, her fingers wrapped around the cold neck of the vodka bottle. Momentarily, she held on to the glass bottle as though her skin was surgically attached, then she opened her fingers one-by-one and pulled her arm back to the boat's lounger.

Damn. Just one drink. It'd been five long years since she'd felt the smooth comfort of cold vodka filling her empty stomach, numbing the pain of everyday life. Five years. She could handle one little swallow.

Her hand reached for the bottle, but instead delivered a hunk of three ice cubes frozen together. She pushed them into her mouth.

A tear rolled from the corner of her eye, down her cheek, and into her ear. She needed a drink. Really needed it. Wanted it more than she wanted to take her next breath. And that's why the seal on the bottle remained intact. Intellectually, she knew the human body didn't require alcohol to survive. Emotionally, she was sure that without a drink within the next five minutes, she would die.

She pulled the bottle from the icy water and sat it on her stomach, watching the clear liquid move sensually around in its container. In the late evening heat, sweat quickly formed on the bottle and soaked through her shirt leaving cold wet rings on her belly.

One drink would extinguish the burning ache in her gut. One drink would get her through tonight and to tomorrow morning. One drink.

Damn Lloyd. She didn't deserve the accusation that she hadn't done her best in the OR. She always did her best.

And damn Monroe too for believing her lying, cheating ex.

She drew in a deep breath and let it out slowly.

Relax. Deep breaths. Concentrate. Feel the gentle rock of the boat.

Well, that new-age crap wasn't helping at all. If having one drink wasn't the answer, then what she really needed was a punching bag with Lloyd's face on one side and Troy Monroe's on the other. On the other hand, Troy looked just like Kyle, and she could never sock him. Another great plan down the drain.

A couple of jet-skis zoomed past, sending her boat rocking like a baby's cradle. Closing her eyes, she thought about her day. It'd started early and run late. Her food intake had been minimal, if you count a candy bar for lunch as food. Face it, she was running on fumes, ready to sputter to a stop any moment.

And she was sad, seriously sad. Losing any patient was bad enough, but a child? Losing a child doubled the melancholy. She no longer had a way to get rid of this much misery. She could cry again, but what good would that do? Tears didn't make her feel any better.

And the vodka? It wouldn't help. She knew that. She shoved the bottle back into the ice chest.

Resting her head on the seatback, she stared at the twinkling lights she'd hung from the boat's metal roof. When lit, the tiny LCD lights put out bright sparkles of light. She loved those lights. They always reminded her of the sparkle in Kyle's eyes when he laughed. His long, lean body when he was naked. The way he strutted instead of walked. Those old jeans that had been washed so many times they were threadbare across his crotch. For the first time today, she felt the corners of her mouth pull upward.

He made her happy. When he was gone, when their affair was over, she would miss him terribly. But in her heart, she knew there would be no husband, no children, no happily-ever-after for her. The best she hoped for in her life was professional success, and now that was being threatened.

In the main channel, a large boat roared past, pulling her from her warm thoughts of Kyle. The racing boat was close enough that his wake sent her boat on another rocking spree. Thank goodness, it hadn't turned into her hiding place. She didn't want strangers intruding on her space.

When the memories of this morning shoved their way to the forefront and she could no longer hold them at bay, she shut her eyes and thought about Hunter Lloyd...his tiny body with its soft skin,; his little chest moving up and down from the respirator in the OR, the seemingly gallons of blood she mopped from inside his abdomen. The tears leaked out, running down her cheeks, and onto her neck.

It wasn't fair. That poor child. That bastard of a father. More concerned about his damn career than his family.

Tess dipped the corner of a towel into the icy water and held it against her swollen eyes.

Maybe she wasn't being fair to Preston. He loved his son. She knew that. This morning's car accident would haunt him the rest of his life. If she were a vindictive woman, she'd take comfort in his pain, but how could anyone take comfort in the loss of a child? She couldn't. She'd been there. Still bore the emotional scars as proof.

Tess rolled to her side on the recliner and refocused her thoughts on Kyle. What was she going to do about him? The longer she continued the affair, the harder and more painful it'd be when he left her.

Did she love him? Without question. She wasn't supposed to fall for the man. Heck, she hadn't even liked him after their first meeting. But when he'd rolled into the emergency department, she'd felt a gut-load of sympathy for him after he'd been shot during a routine traffic stop he'd made on his way home. A car with no tail lights. A simple traffic stop. The worst thing that might have happened to the driver would have been a warning. Instead he'd walked up to a domestic abuse situation that had gone sideways fast.

She rolled onto her back. A cool breeze ruffled her hair, tossing strands across her face. She wanted to brush them back into place, but she was too relaxed to move either of her hands crossed over her waist. Her eyes drifted shut and she smiled as she remembered their first meeting.

It'd been another long day of fighting with hospital administration to get the funding and equipment necessary to adequately equip the operating suites. Then she'd come home to three broken windows and had reported the vandalism to the county sheriff's office.

On the way home after work, Kyle had responded to her nine-one-one call. She'd only found out later that he was the sheriff and not a deputy as she had assumed that night.

She'd been tired and angry and a total bitch. She'd called him a straw-chewing, red-necked, backwoods Barney Fife.

He'd seemed more amused than angry with her totally off-the-mark description. He'd simply shifted the toothpick in his mouth from the right side to the left and grinned. That had made her even madder.

But her bad mood and insults hadn't deterred his investigation. Within a couple of days, three sets of parents hauling three boys—ages six and seven—had stood at her door. The boys had been throwing rocks at her house as target practice before the start of baseball. She'd received profound apologies, checks from the parents, and a month of weed-pulling from the three boys. Now ages eight and nine, the boys could be found at her house as often as their own.

Not the best of beginnings to be sure, but that straw-chewing, red-necked, Barney Fife sure had worked his way into her life and into her heart.

She heard a boat approaching, but didn't bother opening her eyes. Whoever it was could find another cove on the lake. She was here first and had -claimed this one.

The motor slowed and her boat rocked from the new arrival's wake. Bastards. Couldn't they see this spot was taken?

She forced open her eyes, ready to run off the intruders, but the blue light bar on the boat took the words from her mouth. Kyle stood on the front of the marine patrol boat. The boat idled close and Kyle, as comfortable on water as on land, easily jumped onto the front deck of her pontoon boat, sending it rocking again. His cowboy-booted feet landed with a solid thud.

"Thanks, Barr. I'll take it from here."

Kyle opened the swing gate and clomped his way through the boat. Tess rolled to her side, propping her head in the palm of her hand.

"Dr. Sweeney," Kyle said with a grin and touch of his fingers to the brim of his hat.

"Sheriff Monroe. How goes the lake wars?"

"Wet." He laughed at his own joke for a moment before his face fell into a serious expression. "I've been worried about you. Why haven't you returned my calls?"

She rolled onto her back and closed her eyelids, breaking eye contact. Shrugging, she replied, "Busy day."

The boat rocked as Kyle joined her. Those cowboy boots were as out of place on her boat as her flip-flops would be on Kyle's ranch.

His heat and scent wafted around her. Even with her eyes shut, she'd swear she could feel his gaze on her. She glanced up and into his haunting face. "Why are you here, Kyle?"

His stare left her face to pan over the ice chest holding the bottle of vodka before returning to her. "Like I said, I was concerned."

She drew in a deep breath. "It's not been opened. You can check if you want."

"Tess."

He said her name with such emotion, such caring, she almost broke into tears. "You know, don't you?"

"It doesn't matter," he said. "Just shows me once again what a strong woman you are. Lean up."

When she did, he threw one leg over the recliner and dropped into the seat behind her. Then he wrapped her in his arms and pulled her tight against his chest. She settled between his thighs and leaned heavily against his broad, firm body. Her head rose and fell with his quiet breathing. His heart thumped in her ear. The aroma of morning cologne was faint, but she could still smell its spicy allure. She sighed, relaxed and enjoyed being held by this strong man.

They sat in silence for a long time. The horizon turned pinkish-orange, then orange, and then the sun dropped behind the mountains. Evening stars popped bright in the inky sky like tiny flashlights in the dark.

Kyle's lips pressed into the spot behind her right ear. "Ready to talk?"

She rolled her head from side to side on his chest. "Not really." Then she sighed again. "You know about the booze, don't you?"

"Know and gossip are two different things. I only *know* what you've told me. Look at me."

Craning her head to look over her shoulder, she said, "You should get far, far away from me, Kyle. I'm toxic." She turned back to face the water. "You're a good—no, a wonderful man. You deserve more than I can give."

He pulled her tight. "What a pile of dog crap."

"I'm serious."

"Me too, babe. I'm not going anywhere."

She snorted. "You are the most bull-headed man."

"Yup. So start talking. I know you're bummed about the Lloyd kid from this morning, but you've lost patients before. He isn't the first, and I doubt he'll be the last. Why is this one hitting you so hard?"

What could she say? *My ex-lover thinks I killed his son out of spite?*

"And, yes, I know about my jackass of a brother. But he'll come around and see how wrong he is." He kissed her neck. "There'll be days like this. I want to be there for you when they are."

Tess fought the tears welling up in her eyes and swallowed hard. Would he feel the same if he knew everything about her past? The decisions she'd made? The effect they'd had on her?

"Tess. Look at me."

She rolled over until she was lying in his lap looking into his face.

"This just isn't the loss of a patient or my brother, is it?"

She shook her head, swallowing the heavy tang from

nausea coating the back of her throat, the instant flow of saliva on either side of her tongue.

"Trust me."

But deep down, there was no doubt what was causing the nausea. It was time, time to tell Kyle everything. She didn't want to. As soon as she did, she knew their lives would change. A man like him deserved better than her, someone who could give him the family and children he wanted so badly. A woman without her past. She pressed her face into his chest.

"Look at me," he said. His voice was commanding, and she obeyed, pulling her face away from the comfort of his warmth.

"Tell me about you and Lloyd." She must have paled or flinched, because he said, "I've heard the rumors. I know you two have a past, but I want to know the truth, not the idle chatter of bored clerks."

Tess's heart rolled at his words. The nauseating tang in her mouth worsened. She pushed away and stood. Kyle caught her hand and squeezed. In support, she suspected, but there was nothing he could do that would make this any easier. She glanced down at their connected hands, sighed, kissed their interlaced fingers, and then pulled her hand away. She walked across the boat, keeping her back to him. This'd be easier if she didn't have to look at him—as if anything could make it easier.

She took a deep breath and began. "Six years ago, Preston was separated from his wife. They were well on their way to divorce, or at least that's what he told me. We met and were a lit match to a pile of dry leaves. Instant combustion. I was so young. Alone in the big city with no family and only a few friends. I was flattered when he choice me."

Her knuckles whitened as she grasped the railing for support. "Looking back, we'd have burned out fairly quickly.

But while it lasted..." She shrugged. "Well, you know how the early days of lust can be. We were young, thought we had the world by the balls." She released the railing, paced a couple of steps away and then back. Never did she look at him. She couldn't. If he wasn't wearing a look of disgust yet, he would be in a minute. She had no doubt about that.

"We were all young once. Hell, Tess, at our ages, we all have a past. You don't have to go on. I get the picture. You and Lloyd had an affair. So—"

"Wait!" Tess said, interrupting him. "There's more and," she paused, slapped at the tears on her cheeks and continued. "I want you to hear it all."

"But—"

"No!" She risked a glance over her shoulder. "Let me finish."

He nodded and leaned against the seatback and gave her a go-on wave.

"His wife isn't a strong person. She'd built her life and future around being Mrs. Preston Lloyd." She gave a quiet laugh. "But I think I might have underestimated her. She talked Preston into going to her parents' house for the Christmas holidays. Seems she hadn't told her parents that she and Preston were separated and discussing divorce. She begged him to keep up the front for her parents through Christmas. Preston agreed, but I believe it was because her father was bankrolling his run for prosecuting attorney more than it was any type of devotion to Constance. But he went. Told me they slept in the same room but nothing happened."

She paused to sniff. These memories stung her heart. Telling Kyle this story, letting him know how stupid she'd been, tied her guts into knots. Her whole body tingled with embarrassment of her foolish belief in Preston's declarations of love.

"After the first of the year, we took up pretty much where

we left off. Then in mid-February, Constance called with the news that she was pregnant. Preston was thrilled. He could just picture the *little Preston* she was carrying. He told me he loved me and all, but, gee, his wife was pregnant and he felt a sense of responsibility since he was the father after all." Tess paused to draw in a couple of deep breaths, struggling to control the pain of her heart attempting to carve its way out of her chest. "Well, he moved home. Two weeks later, I found out I was pregnant." She waited for Kyle to say something, but he didn't.

He moved to her side and wrapped her in his arms. Over her shoulder she gave him a wan smile, and then turned away and took a few steps away out of his arms. She couldn't look at him. Not yet. Not with what was to come. Gastric acid bubbled in her stomach, burning her throat as it sloshed its way toward her mouth. She forced it back down with a vigorous swallow.

"I'm not done, Kyle. Sit. Let me finish."

Rolling her eyes skyward, she blinked quickly, trying to stem the tears.

"Okay."

The boat rocked as he took two steps back to his seat. Her stomach swayed in time with the boat, worsening her growing nauseous state.

"I didn't tell Preston I was pregnant. For a while, I wasn't sure what to do." She wrapped her arms around her waist, gathering her strength for the next painful segment. Her heart thudded with fear of Kyle's reaction to the rest of her story.

"Somehow, he found out. I think from my doctor. I can't be sure, but they were poker buddies." She dropped her arms down to her side and shrugged. Sighing, she continued. "Doesn't matter how. The important thing is he did find out and came to my house late one night. Demanded to know if it was true..if I pregnant with his child? At first, I lied and told him it was another man's child. He didn't believe me. He'd kept track of me even after he'd moved home. Knew I hadn't been seeing anyone else. He kept on badgering and badgering me until I finally admitted the baby I carried was his."

She wrung her hands. The view in front of her blurred from the unshed tears. Sniffing, she continued. "He told me to get an abortion. Said he wouldn't have bastard children running ruining his good name." She choked on her snicker. "His good name. What a joke. I told him I would, but—" She swung around to glance at Kyle, to see his face, to see his reaction. He gave her the continue wave, so she did. "I didn't. Have an abortion, I mean. What I knew was that I would never abort my child. Lloyd didn't know that about me. For all I knew, the baby I carried might be the only child I would ever have. I decided to move away. Have the child and never tell him."

Catching his gaze for just a moment before turning back to face the water, she said, "I would be a good mother. I know I would." Then her shoulders sagged from the weight of the story. "So a couple of weeks later, I called his office and told him I'd had an abortion. The bastard mailed me a check for five hundred dollars. I tore it into little pieces and mailed it back." She smiled, remembering how good it had felt to shove his precious money back in his face, even if it turned had out to be a major mistake on her part.

"So, where's the child?" Kyle asked in a quiet voice.

This time, there was no holding back the tears. Her eyes simply overflowed. "I lost the baby. When Preston got the torn-up check pieces back, he came to my house. He was furious. Out of his mind. He knew I hadn't gone through with an abortion. He...he hit me. Slapped me, first. Knocked me into a table. I tried to protect my baby the best I could. He said if I had this baby, he'd make sure the courts knew how unfit I was as a mother. He'd take the child and put it up for adoption."

"That sonofabitch hit you? Now you've given me another reason I need to kill the bastard. You should have called the cops, babe."

"I couldn't. I was scared to death of him, so I ran. What else could I do? I had nothing. No money. No job. Huge medical school bills. Nobody I could turn to for help. The closest large medical community was Memphis, so I headed there to look for other job opportunities. Two days after I got there, I began bleeding. There was nothing anyone could do. The baby, my son, was too small, too premature. There were complications with the delivery. Some excess bleeding. Some damage to my uterus."

She hiccupped, then turned to face him, terrified that she'd just destroyed her future, their future. The muscles in her legs threatened to give way. She leaned on the boat's side rail for support.

"So that's why Preston thinks I killed his son this morning, as sort of a get-back-at-him move, I guess." Looking over her shoulder, she said, "I didn't. I wouldn't."

Kyle walked to her and enfolded her in his arms. "Good lord almighty, Tess. I know you wouldn't. You don't have it in you to kill. The man's an asshole and a liar."

"Liar?"

"Come here and sit. Let me tell you what I know."

They resumed their positions on the boat's recliner...him in the back, her sitting between his legs. He pulled her against him again.

"I'm pretty sure Lloyd was at fault for the accident."

"Why? How do you know?"

"I don't yet, but we'll get to the bottom of this. What we do know is that no child booster seat has been found, not at the scene, and so far, not in Ten Mile River. I think Lloyd's lying. I think his son was asleep in the back seat unrestrained. I think Lloyd was driving drunk. When the two cars hit, I think his son was thrown from the car as he said, but I don't believe the booster-seat nonsense."

"Oh," she said, sitting up. "Let me say that I'm pretty sure the Worthington kid wasn't drinking and hadn't taken any drugs. Off the record, there was nothing at all in his blood. I had to take him to surgery this morning for a chest tube and I had to know. I'm not telling you this, of course."

"Of course," Kyle said. "Never heard a thing, but thanks. I can get those hospital records if we need them."

"Good," she said, settling back against his chest feeling a tad guilty she hadn't told him the whole story about the miscarriage and her probable infertility. But for now, for tonight, she'd take the comfort he was offering and deal with the rest of her history later.

"So, as I was saying, I don't believe for one minute that your abilities had anything to do with the child's death, and I told my brother that tonight."

She flinched at the mention of Troy Monroe. "Yes, well, your brother isn't my biggest fan."

"And he should be," he said. "You saved my life. He should be offering you a lifetime appointment."

She shrugged. "Not all men like the idea of female surgeons. Somehow we are a threat to their masculinity."

"That's crazy."

"Maybe, but I've still faced it for years." She turned to look at him. "You didn't tell him about us, right? I mean, that could do nothing to help."

"I've told him nothing." He leaned forward and kissed her. His lips were warm and soft. His tongue traced her bottom lip and she opened to let him in. He stroked along the edge of hers as their two tongues tangled. When the kiss finally ended, he pressed his forehead against hers. "But I think it's time to go public."

"No! Not now." She pulled back. "You're up for reelection. Lloyd is out for blood. He can go after me. That's fine. I can take it, but I won't let him ruin you too in the process of trying to take me down. No way."

"My tough gal," he said with a chuckle.

"I'm serious, Kyle."

"Me too, babe. Serious about you. And I want the whole world, or at least our little corner of the world to know."

"Kyle..."

He kissed her again, this time long and slow and deep. While his hands slipped under her T-shirt and his thick fingers caressed her breasts, she sighed.

She nibbled and kissed along his jaw until she reached his ear. Using the tip of her tongue, she traced the outer fold of his ear. "Not fair," she whispered in his ear. She felt the tremor as it shook him, and she smiled. Soft words in his ear were one of his definite weaknesses. "You know I can't think when you touch me like that."

Returning her torture with a little of his own, he pushed her bra up to fondle her, skin touching skin, one of her weaknesses. "I don't play fair when there's something I want," he whispered in her ear, sending an army of goose bumps marching down her spine. "And you, lady, are something I want."

She struggled out of his arms and stood. "I...I'm developing feelings."

"Feelings? Hell, Tess. I'm falling in love with you."

His words, which should have made her happy, instead stirred up a sadness down deep.

"You need to hear the rest of the story."

"Whatever it is, it won't matter. We'll face it together."

CHAPTER EIGHT

Preston's day pretty much went to hell the minute he got out of bed. Constance had sniffed and whimpered all night. He'd barely gotten any sleep at all.

When they'd arrived at Diamond Lakes Funeral Home to make arrangements, he was stunned to discover his son's body hadn't been released yet. Another example of the ineptitude of the local medical community. Regardless, they had an appointment with the funeral director, and Preston was nothing if not a man of his word.

His wife had been no help at all in planning Hunter's funeral. She'd spent the entire time crying and going through tissues like she did his money. The brainless twit didn't seem to realize that Hunter was his son also and maybe, just maybe, he was suffering too and could use some support. But no. It was all about her and her grief. Heaven forbid anyone give him a thought.

Arrangements made, he'd dropped his wife off at home and told her he was going to the office for a couple of hours. She'd just nodded and gone inside their house. He'd shaken his head in disgust at his clueless spouse. What grieving father would go to the office on the same day he made funeral arrangement for his only son?

He'd driven over to his girlfriend's house. Deidra would understand what he was going through. She always did. Plus, she'd know exactly who to contact at the newspaper to drop a discrete whisper about an alcoholic doctor practicing at St. Michael's.

He made a mental note to speak with Sheriff Monroe. Even though the state police was in charge of the accident investigation, Monroe was up for reelection and Preston was sure Monroe could use some of his influence and money. In return, Monroe would put a word in with the state police and the accident report would say what it was supposed to.

After all, any sheriff worth his salt would want a good working relationship with the prosecuting attorney.

And while he was thinking about it, he needed to get his secretary to make a lunch date with the Dallas regional representative for the Texas State Police. Since it was a female, he was fairly certain, as far as the accident report went, that he could get her to see his version of events from that night.

As he lay in Deidra's bed while she gave him a blow-job, his mind continued to throw ideas at him, ideas on how to get both Tess and Candy McCall out of his life in one fell swoop... two birds, one stone, so to speak. Dangerous, yes, but also so brilliant he couldn't believe he hadn't thought of it until now. What if Tess shot Candy, a disgruntled, rejected old lover shooting the new lover? Or better yet, what if Tess shot Candy as payback to the hospital chairman for not backing her in this latest fiasco with Hunter? Either way, he was the prosecuting attorney. He could frame the case however he wanted. Hell, he even knew where Tess kept her gun. Bedside table, right side.

Now to get Candy to Tess's house for the final act.

Holding Deidra's head firmly, he thrust down her throat until he came with a grunt and groan.

"Good one, baby," he said. "Love you loads."

CHAPTER NINE

On Monday morning, Tess woke to thunderstorms and pouring rain. Like she'd done since she was a child, she slid back under the covers, pulling them up to her chin and lying there enjoying the cracks of lightning and the booms of thunder. When her phone alarm gonged, she sighed and rolled over to grab it off her table. After hitting snooze at least three times, she pulled herself from bed and headed for the shower. She had surgery this morning, and if she could make up the snooze time, she might be able to do her rounds before then.

As she pulled from the driveway, she opened her door far enough to snag the plastic-covered Diamond Lakes Times. She wedged it between her seat and the door. No time to read it this morning.

She walked into the surgery suite at six a.m. The usually friendly staff was subdued. No one wanted to meet her gaze. Oh, they replied when she said "good morning," but they quickly went back to whatever they were doing. It even appeared the staff were lookng for something to do rather than chat with her.

"Morning, Tess."

Tess turned and smiled at Guy Madison. "Good morning, Guy. Did you have a nice weekend?"

He raised one eyebrow. "Have you seen today's paper?"

"No. I was running a little late this morning. Why?"

He hooked his arm through hers. "Come with me."

"What's going on?"

Guy didn't answer. He led her to the physicians' lounge, which happened to be empty at the moment.

"You need to read the article on the first page."

"Why? What does it say?"

Below the fold was an article about an unnamed female surgeon accused of operating on a child while under the influence. The article didn't name Tess, but she was the only female surgeon on staff at St. Michael's. It wouldn't take a genius to know who the paper was referring to. But where did they get their information?

As she read the account of Friday night's tragic accident—which put blame solely on the Freddy Worthington—Tess could see Preston's fingerprints all over. This was, without doubt, his version of the story. He knew about her history with alcohol. He knew too many of the details in the story for him not to be the unnamed source close to the investigation. Bastard.

"Son of a bitch," she muttered.

"It's libel, pure and simple." Guy rubbed her shoulders. "I know that's all bullshit. So does every person in the room that night. Lloyd ought to know better than this."

"Maybe, but where's his name in this article, other than as a victim from the accident and the grieving father of a dead son? I'll never prove he talked to the press. Never. You know how they protect their sources."

The door to the lounge opened and head nurse Kelly Franco entered.

"Good morning, Doctors. Dr. Sweeney. I need to have a word please."

"I'll go," Guy said.

"No, stay," Tess said, wondering if she would need a witness for this conversation latter.

Kelly Franco sighed. "I am so sorry, Dr. Sweeney. Your patients for this morning have requested another physician do their surgeries."

Tess stumbled backwards, prevented from falling only when Guy caught her shoulders. "Excuse me?"

Kelly shrugged. "I think it was the article in the paper. One patient withdrew his permission for surgery. Another called this morning to reschedule. I just hung up the phone after talking with your third scheduled patient, who voiced concern over the article in the paper. I assured her the paper had it wrong, but..." A sheepish expression flashed across her face. "She's asked for a different surgeon. Are you aware that Dr. Monroe has asked to meet with the staff who worked with you this past weekend?"

Tess massaged her neck, which did nothing for the tension building there. "No, but I'm not surprised. Internal investigation, huh?"

"I haven't been notified," Guy said.

"You will be," Kelly said. "Have you checked your emails?"

"No." He pulled a cell phone from his front pocket and loaded his most recent messages. "Damnation." He clicked, read, and then gave another, "Damnation. It's here."

"I'm sorry." Kelly's face was a mask of embarrassment and pity. It was the pity that almost did Tess in.

"Don't worry about it. I hate you're being drawn into something like this when neither of you deserve it. I'm sure it'll all be worked out."

Damn Preston. If she could only change the past.

Tess rearranged the strap of her tote bag. "Thanks for

letting me know about my patients. I'll go do my rounds now." She left the doctors' lounge with her head held high. She wasn't going to let that SOB Lloyd make her cry.

The hospital floors were alive with residents and medical students making rounds, updating charts, and giving reports to attending physicians. She pulled Freddy Worthington's chart, checked his latest vital signs and lab reports and headed for his room. She knocked then entered. Judge Worthington stood when she entered.

"Good morning," she said, forcing a cheerfulness she didn't feel into her voice. "How's our patient today?"

"Morning, Dr. Sweeney. He's doing good."

Freddy was still asleep, which wasn't surprising given the early hour.

"His lab reports are good. How's he doing with the insulin injections?"

The judge smiled. "Better than I thought."

"I can answer for myself," a groggy voice retorted.

"Morning, sunshine," Tess said. She stepped closer to the bed. "How are you feeling?"

Freddy pushed himself upright. "Better. I hate those shots, but I feel a lot better than I have in a while."

"Good. From my standpoint, I have no reason to keep you any longer. I'm discharging you from my care. If your internist agrees, I think you'll go home today." She smiled. "I'm glad you weren't hurt too badly on Friday night. Take care."

"Thank you, Dr. Sweeney," Freddy said.

"You're very welcome."

"Dr. Sweeney," Judge Worthington said. "Can I have a word with you outside?"

"Certainly. Nice to meet you, Freddy."

Fred Worthington followed her into the hall. He wasted

no time getting to his point. "I assume you've seen today's newspaper."

Tess's gut rolled with anxiety. "I have."

"It's all bullshit."

She nodded. "I know it and you know it, but the public?" She shrugged. "It'll be front page today with the retraction or story correction on page five in a few days."

"I'm not sure. I've had Lloyd in my court. He's like a pitbull when he gets his mind set. I think you'd better get yourself a lawyer."

"Thanks, Judge, but I don't think it'll go that far."

Worthington pulled his business card from his pocket. On the back he'd written a name and phone number. "Call this guy. Best criminal attorney in the state."

She took the card, still sure she'd never need it. "Really, I appreciate your concern, but I'm sure this will die out soon."

He took her hand and held it for a minute. "You probably saved my son's life. I'll always be in your corner. If you need anything, and I mean anything, don't hesitate to call. My home and office numbers are on that card. I'm serious, Dr. Sweeney. Call me."

She put the card in her pocket. "Thanks, Judge. I appreciate your concern."

By the time she reached her office, she wasn't sure if she should be concerned that Judge Worthington thought she needed a lawyer...and a criminal one at that. Her phone beeped a text message alarm before she could unlock her door. Expecting it to be Kyle, she was surprised at the message.

MEET ME IN MY OFFICE AT EIGHT A.M.

TROY MONROE

Well, crap. Nothing good ever came out of that man's mouth or his office. It was seven-thirty, and with no surgery today, she had time to brew a cup of coffee for her caffeine fix.

At five minutes to eight, she walked into the chief of staff's office. His secretary hadn't arrived yet, but his door was ajar. She wasn't one to pry, but it was difficult when angry male voices were so clearly audible.

"This is a hospital matter. You have no business sticking your nose in."

"I know Tess Sweeney. She wouldn't operate if she'd been drinking."

"I understand why you'd support her. She did your surgery six months ago. You feel indebted to her. I get that, but Friday was a totally different situation. I can't have an impaired surgeon operating. I just can't. Hell, the gossip about the embezzlement under the last administration is just dying down, not to mention the firestorm about those pictures of the OB residents having basically a sex orgy in the on-call rooms. No. I have to nip this in the bud."

"She wasn't drinking on Friday. Trust me."

"And you know this how?"

Tess knocked on the door, interrupting before Kyle could speak. "Good morning. I believe we have an appointment at eight."

Troy Monroe glared at her like she was dog poop on the bottom of his shoe. "This is a private conversation, Dr. Sweeney. You can wait outside."

"No, I don't think so," Tess said, walking into Monroe's office. "If it were that private, your door should have been shut." She closed the door firmly. "There. Now it's private. However, I was unaware we had a criminal situation that required bringing in Sheriff Monroe."

Kyle took a step toward her, but she stopped him with a look.

"Not criminal, or at least not yet," Troy Monroe said. "As

you are fully aware, operating under the influence is a serious charge, a criminal charge."

"And yet, you have only the word of a grieving father who most likely contributed to his son's death."

Troy's gaze slid to his brother and back to Tess. "Whether Lloyd was at fault totally, or even played a contributing factor, in the death of his son isn't our concern." He waved to the chair in front of his desk. "Please sit."

"No, thank you. I believe I'll stand."

The Monroe twins were too much of Southern gentlemen to sit while she stood, so they remained standing.

"Fine. As you know, Preston Lloyd has reported you to this office, to the hospital's chairman of the board, and the Texas State Medical Board. In his complaint, he alleges you performed surgery on his son while intoxicated."

Tess crossed her arms. "And that is bullshit."

Troy shrugged. "Maybe. Maybe not. The problem is your alcoholic addiction history. Ninety percentage of alcoholics relapse, and that's his assertion."

She stiffed her back. "Probably closer to fifty or sixty."

"Still, I can't take the chance, especially since you're not only on staff but in a position of authority."

Kyle stepped forward. Tess's gaze whipped toward him and she narrowed her eyes in a warning to stay quiet. Either her glare needed work or he simply ignored her.

"She wasn't drunk," he growled at his brother.

"Kyle…" Tess rested her hand on his forearm. "Let it go."

"I won't," he said, putting his hand over hers.

"What's going on here?" Troy asked, his eyes wide with disbelief.

"I'll tell him." Tess faced Troy Monroe. "Your brother and I have been seeing each other for the past eight weeks or so."

"Is this true, Kyle?"

"Yup." He squeezed Tess's hand. "I've wanted to tell you,

but Tess didn't want you to think she was courting favors with you by dating your brother."

Troy gave a harsh laugh. "I'm sure. Good Lord, Dr. Sweeney. Dating a patient. Is there any medical standard you won't break?"

"He was long discharged from my care before we had our first date. There was no medical tenet broken."

"So my brother is your alibi for Friday night? He's the proof you weren't been drinking? An ex-patient who owes you his life and has publically stated he's indebted to you? An ex-patient you're now sleeping with? I assume you are sleeping together."

Tess's nose rose a little. "We take a break from fucking to sleep every now and then."

A red flush rose up Troy's neck to his face.

"Tess." Kyle put his arm around her shoulders. "Troy. She wasn't drinking on Friday or any night that we've been together. I've never seen her take as much as a sip of alcohol. As I tried to tell you on Friday, you're backing the wrong horse if you put your chips on Lloyd. He's a liar, a womanizer, and probably guilty of his son's death."

Troy dropped heavily into the large, leather chair behind his desk. "Fuck. Fuck. Fuck."

Tess and Kyle exchanged glances, and then Tess walked over to the edge of Troy's desk.

"I'm assuming there is an autopsy being done on Hunter Lloyd?"

"Yes. I ordered one as soon as Lloyd left my office on Friday."

"I'm sure it will back me up regarding the severity of his injuries. There's nothing I can do to prove there was no alcohol or other drug in my bloodstream that night."

"I'm interviewing the OR staff you worked with that night."

Tess nodded. "Good. And talk to Judge Fred Worthington and his wife. I spent a lot of time with them."

"True, but at least a couple of hours had passed since you arrived at the hospital."

"Fine, do whatever you need, but I'm telling you, I wasn't drunk."

"And I'm backing her up," Kyle said from behind her.

"Until this issue is resolved, I think it best if you take a couple of days leave."

Tess placed her hands on his desk and leaned forward. "You're putting me on leave?"

"Yes, pending the outcome of my internal investigation."

"You're such an ass, Monroe. Your own brother backs my story."

"My brother's head has been turned by a pretty woman before."

"Hey!" Kyle said. "I won't have you questioning me or Tess regarding our honesty."

Troy shrugged. "Until I have a decision, Dr. Sweeney, please let your staff handle your cases. I understand you had some cancellations this morning?"

Tess's head almost split from grinding her teeth. "Yes."

"Exactly," Troy said smugly.

"I will not take a leave of absence. That's as much as an admission of guilt. I have plenty of administrative work to keep me busy."

"Fine, but no patient care until the situation has been resolved."

"I don't think you're being fair, Troy," Kyle said. "Tess is totally innocent here."

"Then my investigation will bear that out."

"Is that all?" Tess asked, her lips pulling into a tight line.

"That's it."

Tess turned on her heel and marched from the office, the anger inside growing like a stoked furnace.

"Tess. Wait." Kyle hurried after her. When he reached for her, she stepped away.

"I think it might be better if we didn't see each other for a while," she said. "There's no reason to give Lloyd another target for his revenge."

"Don't be ridiculous."

"I'm not being ridiculous. I'm being sensible. You're up for reelection against one of your own deputies. Lloyd wants this to be nasty. I don't want you sucked into my cesspool."

"Tess, babe–"

"Please, Kyle. Don't make this harder on me than it already is. I can't worry about you while I'm treading professional water." She kissed him. "Understand I'm doing this for both of us."

She rushed into the hall and down the staircase before he could follow.

————

KYLE'S GUT TWISTED. Damn woman was going to drive him nuts. He glanced at his brother's office door but decided any other discussions about Tess's state on Friday night would be fruitless.

And if Tess thought he would walk away from her willingly, she had it all wrong.

As he headed for the hospital exit, he pulled his cell phone from his pocket. "Adam. Any luck finding that missing booster seat from the Lloyd accident?"

"No, sir. Vaughn and I have been up and down the creek. Found lots of trash but no booster seat."

"Have we heard anything back from Sheriff Singer whether anything was found in Whispering Springs County?"

"Not yet, sir."

"I'll call Singer."

"Thanks, sir. And I had another idea."

Kyle slid his sunglasses on to block out the bright Texas sun. "Okay. Shoot."

"My nephew's boy scout troop is working on badges. I was thinking they could do a Ten Mile River clean-up project. Maybe the department could supply a deputy or two to work with them. Make a big deal out of it."

Kyle smiled. "That's a great idea. We'll donate those bright orange bags the department has."

"Thanks, Sheriff. I'll call my brother tonight."

"Great. Keep me in the loop."

Deep in his soul, Kyle knew the clean-up wouldn't produce that missing booster seat because he was sure there was no missing seat.

CHAPTER TEN

Kyle called Tess when he got back to his car and wasn't surprised when she didn't pick up. She was, without doubt, the most bullheaded woman he knew, and yet, there was a kindness in her soul outside of medicine that she didn't show many people. He'd seen it when he'd awoke after surgery with the ever-so-proper Dr. Sweeney sitting by his bed, his hand grasped in both of hers. Of course, she'd immediately jerked her hand away and started taking his pulse. His heart warmed at the memory.

When her voice mail message instructed him to leave a message, he said, "Hey, babe. Don't let my brother or that ass Lloyd get you down. I'm here for you. We'll come out the other side. Talk to you later." He paused and then added, "Love you, Tess."

A couple of minutes after he disconnected, his phone dinged with a text message.

I NEED SOME TIME. PLEASE DON'T CALL ME. AND PLEASE, DON'T LOVE ME. BETTER YET, MOVE ON. FIND SOMEONE ELSE. I CAN'T DRAG YOU INTO MY MESS.

Silly woman. Find someone else? Why would he do that after he'd had the best in her?

Nonetheless, he'd give her a couple of days. It wasn't as if he didn't have enough to do to get the bottom of everything. He wondered if Lloyd had any past driving infractions, especially a DUI.

He started his truck and headed for his office. At least he had something he could do.

———

THE NEXT COUPLE of days passed in a haze of internet searches, paperwork, and general sheriff office drudgery. Of course, the numerous mutilated and spray-painted Kyle Monroe for Sherriff signs were a little different. He had his suspicions about who was behind the destruction of his signs but for now he let it go.

Tess never called. That didn't shock him. He sent her a text every night with the same general message.

MISS YOU. LOVE YOU. I'M HERE WHEN YOU'RE READY.

Apparently, she wasn't ready. That was okay. It'd taken him thirty-eight years to find the right woman, plus months of asking her out before she accepted. He could wait for her to realize he wasn't going anywhere.

On Thursday, Sheriff Singer called from the next county over. The local judge and he had rounded up some nonviolent law breakers who were happy to clean Ten Mile River for time served. To no one's surprise, no child booster seat was found. Lots of trash, a couple of waterlogged tired, and even one old bicycle, but no child seat.

The state police had assigned a special prosecutor to the case, making sure this would drag on forever. In some way, Kyle wished he still had the case. On the other hand, he wanted

Lloyd to go down for killing his son. Even Kyle could see that he had a conflict of interest. No doubt Lloyd's attorney would have used that conflict to stir up all kinds of doubts.

Friday started off like every other day that day. No calls nor messages from Tess. He wasn't surprised. The local news rag had run daily articles about the tragic death of Hunter Lloyd. Local, and then national news outlets had picked up the story of the death and accusations of an impaired doctor performing surgery. However, the national news outlets had used the story to do in-depth reminders to parents on the need for car seats for children.

Today would be the last day Kyle was going to allow radio silence to continue. Maybe this afternoon, he would kidnap Tess away to the family ranch and grab them a couple of horses. Nobody could stay in a bad mood on the back of smooth riding quarter horse.

"Sheriff." The desk clerk shoved her head into his office. "Your brother is on line three."

"Thanks." Kyle lifted the receiver. "Troy. What's up?"

"Thought maybe you'd meet me for a late lunch, say about one?"

"Sure. Where?"

"The Water's Edge work for you?"

Kyle shook his head. His brother was on the prowl for some weekend companionship. Kyle didn't miss that scene at all. Tess was the only woman he needed for the rest of his life.

"Sure. See you there."

At a little after one, he pulled into the Water's Edge and parked next to his brother's black Mercedes coupe. That car probably cost twice as much as Kyle made in a year as sheriff, not that his salary was all that important to him. His maternal grandparents had done quite well in the oil business, leaving Kyle and his four siblings quite comfortable financially. Only his younger brother had flittered away a portion of his inheritance, but Beau had wised up before his entire nest egg was gone. Kyle rarely touched his trust fund. The nice thing about having money was knowing it was there if he needed it but not really requiring it to live. He did fine on his sheriff's pay.

Troy was seated at a window table, his hand wrapped around a dewy glass of iced tea. Kyle was taken aback to see his other siblings around the table. He laughed to himself. An intervention was his guess.

"Good afternoon, family," he said, dropping into the one vacant chair. "This is a surprise. Are we having a family meeting?"

He let his gaze fall on his sister, Risa...the weakest link when it came to keeping secrets.

"Um," Risa said. "Troy thought—"

Troy cleared his throat.

"I mean, we thought maybe we should talk about your job."

Kyle arched an eyebrow. "My job?" His gaze slid over to his youngest brother. "Really, Beau? You're worried about my job?"

A flush climbed up Beau's neck. "Um, we..." He looked at Troy and back. "We know how much you like being sheriff and would hate if, um, something were to interfere with that."

Beside him, Troy lifted his sweat-laden iced-tea glass to his lips, his hands as steady as a rock. Kyle loved his family but obviously his twin hadn't given up the notion of getting Tess out of his life.

"I'm guessing that you've all seen the newspaper articles this week," Troy said, then dapped his cloth napkin to his lips.

Kyle glared at his siblings, intimidating only the youngest three. Troy met Kyle's glare with a sarcastic lift of his eyebrow.

"Dr. Sweeney is being not only a pain in my ass, but she's become a real liability to the hospital."

The waitress came by and Kyle ordered coffee. Although he was sorely tempted to walk out, that wouldn't solve anything. Maybe if he stayed, he could get his three younger siblings into his boat and the four of them could tell Troy to go jump in the lake.

"Let me tell you all something," Kyle said. He leaned on the table and aimed a particularly mean glare at his twin. "If I have anything to say about it, Tess Sweeney will be around in this town and in my life forever. *Forever.* Get it?"

His brother Heath nodded. "Good. I like Dr. Sweeney. Hell, the whole family owes her for saving your worthless hide. I tried to tell Mr. High and Mighty here"—he indicated Troy with a lift of his chin—"that he was barking up the wrong tree both with this family meeting and with trying to get Dr. Sweeney fired. Go on, Dr. Jackass. Tell our brother what your little hospital investigation showed."

Troy's back stiffened.

"Let me guess," Kyle said. "You found she did nothing wrong."

"Well, I'll just say that the staff couldn't confirm nor deny whether she'd been drinking that night."

"Bullshit." Kyle slapped the table top and shoved his chair back with a loud screech on the wooden plank floor to stand. "I can, and you don't trust me? I told you I'd been with her all evening. She hadn't had a drop to drink."

Around them, other late lunch patrons were beginning to turn toward the noise.

"Sit down," Beau said. "Don't make a scene."

"Which is exactly why we met here, isn't it? So you could try to control me?"

"Please sit down, Kyle," Risa said. "Please."

Kyle sat, but the gritting of his teeth was starting to give him a major headache. "Troy. I'm warning you. If you do anything to Tess, I will never speak to you again in this lifetime."

Troy rolled his eyes. "Please. So dramatic over some woman."

"That's enough," Heath said. "You two may be three years older than me but you're acting like a couple of high schoolers." He turned to Kyle. "I don't think the rest of us were aware of how serious you'd become about Dr. Sweeney. Troy said you had a mild infatuation, but I'm thinking he undersold what's going on."

"Well now you know. One of these days, I'm going to marry that woman, so he—and you three—need to understand that." He looked at Troy. "Weren't you going to order an autopsy?"

"Lloyd didn't want one done."

Kyle snorted. "I bet he didn't"

"Didn't matter. State police ordered one."

"And? Holding out on me, brother?"

Troy blew out a long breath. "Severe trauma from being ejected from the car. Massive internal injuries and bleeding. Basically, it was amazing the kid lived long enough to make it to the OR." He shrugged. "Combined with the staff reports, looks like Sweeney did what she could. I've turned everything over to the state police per their request."

"God, you're a jerk. If you weren't my brother—worse my twin—I'd take you outside to the parking lot and put a dent in that perfect nose of yours."

"I'm just trying to watch out for you."

"Ha." Kyle glanced around at his three other siblings. "What exactly did Troy tell you to get you all here?

Risa leaned on the table. "Not what I'm hearing tonight. Not even close." She held Troy's gaze, apparently not fazed by his glare. "Alcoholic doctor, check. Not serious, check. Probably going to get rid of her from hospital so it'd be better if you moved on, check." She moved her gaze to Beau and then Heath. "The same?"

The two men nodded.

"Then let me be frank. I'm in love with Tess Sweeney. If she'll have me, I plan to marry her."

Surprise opened Risa's eyes wide. "How can you be so serious and not brought her around to meet Mom and Dad?"

"I've met her," Beau said.

"Me, too," said Heath."

"How? When?" Risa demanded.

"She's been riding at the sables for the past year or so. Always requests Blaze," Beau explained. "Since I'm usually in the stables, I take care of her. We"—he indicated Heath with a head tilt—"were a little nervous about giving her Blaze. You know how he can be with new people but he and Tess connected immediately. She saddles Blaze herself and unsaddles and grooms him when she gets back."

"I told her she didn't have to do that," Heath said.

"Well." Troy snorted. "Looks like she had her eyes on our brother for a long time...longer than he even he knew."

"You're way off-base," Kyle said. "She's a rider. There aren't that many stables that rent horses in our area."

"But there are others," Troy said.

"True, but we have the most acreage for riding."

Troy shrugged. "The way I see it, she was planning on worming her way into your life one way or the other. The gunshot was her lucky break."

"I am seriously thinking about busting your lip at the same time I dent that perfect nose of yours if you say another word."

"Hate to say this, Troy, but I'm thinking you sold the three of us a bill of goods on Dr. Sweeney," Beau said.

Risa put her hand on Kyle's wrist. "Bring her to dinner on

Sunday. Let us get to know her as someone other than your doctor and one of our renters."

"Maybe. How do I know he'll behave?" He glared across the table at his twin.

"He will, or *I'll* bust his nose...and you know I can," Risa said.

Kyle rubbed his nose. Risa had busted it with the back of her head when he'd been trying to teach her self-protection. He chuckled. "I remember." He stood. "I'll talk to Mom and Tess about Sunday. Anything else?"

"Yeah," Heath said. "Sorry about the intervention."

Kyle smiled. "Love you guys. I just don't love you guys in my business."

———

THE WEEK ENDED BETTER than it started for Tess, well, until she pulled into her drive Friday afternoon. The *Kyle Monroe for Sheriff* sign had been sprayed with the words *BABY KILLER* in blood red. She sighed, pulled into her garage and went back out to collect it. She'd have to let Kyle know about it.

This wasn't the first mutilated or spray-painted sign she'd seen this week. Not only did this property destruction make her angry, but it embarrassed her that he was catching all the flack because of her. It just wasn't right. He was too good of a man, and a hell of a good sheriff, for her to be casting her negative shadow over. She'd told him to move on and forget her, and she hadn't heard from him in the last couple of days. Had he decided that she was right and being with her was too much trouble? Her gut turned a tad sour at the thought.

She propped the sign in her garage and unlocked the door to her house. Walking in and seeing the sparkle of the lake out the back glass wall always lifted whatever weight was on her shoulders. She sagged against the kitchen counter for a minute and took in the view of boats cutting through the waves, sending glimmering sunshine across the ripples. Sure seemed like the boaters came out earlier and earlier every year.

One more long breath of relaxation and she began to strip off her scrubs and head for the shower. At least her surgery schedule had picked back up, not back to normal, but up. Of course that was probably because Judge Worthington had had a press conference on Wednesday to reaffirm his belief in her and to tell how she'd saved his son's life. Wow, had that set off Preston, or she assumed it was Preston. She'd had hang-up calls all night after that.

The man was losing all sense of right and wrong. Oh, to the outside world he still appeared to be the polished and well-spoken district attorney but she saw through that. In his eyes, she saw the dark madness brewing. Every day she waited for the other shoe to drop but nothing happened.

Out of the shower, she dressed in shorts and a T-shirt, sans bra. Mother Nature had already bumped up the temps and since her nightly plans were a pizza and a book, the less she wore, the cooler she'd be.

After putting her pizza in the oven, she padded barefoot around her kitchen as she brewed a fresh pot of tea to drink with her dinner. She'd just pulled the pizza from the oven when there was a knock at her front door.

When she opened the door, Kyle caught her face in his hands and drew her into a rough, hungry kiss that demanded she respond. She did, grabbing the belt loops of his jeans and pulling him into her house.

He touched the tip of his tongue to her lips, and she opened. He swept in and her knees buckled under the onslaught. She moaned, the sound vibrating deep in her soul. She soaked up his attention like an arid desert in a rainstorm.

Pulling back, he stared into her eyes. "Do not ever let a week pass again that I don't see you."

He left a trail of kisses along her cheek back down to her mouth. She moaned her response, which could have been anything from "No, no, stop," to "Take me to bed now."

As though he heard the second option, he slipped his hands under her T-shirt at her waist and began walking her backwards toward her bedroom.

CHAPTER ELEVEN

Tess's stomach quivered. His fingers were ten lit matches to a brush of dry kindling. Flames of lust shot through her. Heat flared from the top of her head to the bottom of her feet.

"Too slow," Kyle said. He swept her up into his arms and, with long strides, carried her to her bedroom, all the while continuing to make love to her mouth with his tongue.

It was all too much, and at the time, it wasn't enough. Her clothes were too tight, too restrictive. She couldn't breathe. Her heart played her ribs like a xylophone. Could he not hear the loud pound of her heart?

As he lowered her to the floor next to her bed, she slid down his body like an exotic dancer with her pole. He stepped back and looked deeply into her eyes.

"Tell me you want this as much as I do."

With the Cheshire cat smile, she unbuckled his belt, then his jeans, and finally lowered the zipper. A smile pulled at the corner of his lips.

So he thought he was in charge?

Tess plunged her hand under the waistband of his briefs and took the velvety rod into her hands. Kyle sucked in a breath, the smile falling from his mouth as his eyes darkened with desire.

"I think actions speak louder than words, don't you?" she asked, giving his cock a long, firm stroke. And then another

His eyes rolled back in his head before the lids fell. His nostrils flared as he sucked in a long draw of air.

He pulled her hand from his pants. "No more. Not now. Not if you want this to last longer than the next three minutes."

She laughed. "Finger on the trigger, Sheriff?"

"Only with you, love. Only with you."

He pulled her to him for a long kiss, all lips, and tongues, and teeth. They ate at each other's mouths, needing to take as much as they could from the other as if their kisses were the life-sustaining force required to keep living.

"Overdressed for this ballgame," he said, pushing her shorts down her legs.

She jerked her T-shirt over her head.

"Why, you're commando," he observed. "How convenient."

"I try."

Kneeling in front of her, he lifted one foot and then the other, removing her shorts and tossing them in the corner.

"Spread your legs."

Oh man, she loved when he used his take-no-prisoners voice. His sharp command shot a volt of lust through her, ramping up the fluid trickling from her canal.

"Wider."

Holy hell. If he kept this up, her knees were going to give out and she'd collapse to the floor. Still, she did as she asked, separating her feet into a wide-straddled stance.

He blew on her coarse hair and then across her swollen sex.

She shivered as an army of goose bumps slid down her spine.

Nuzzling his nose in close, he inhaled. "Mm. Love the way you smell."

Before she could respond, he darted out his tongue and licked her engorged clitoris. Tess's knees shook.

"Damn. I'm not sure how long I can stand up with you doing that."

"I can fix that." He rose, took her shoulders, and pushed her back on the bed. "Scoot to the edge."

He draped her legs over his shoulders and found where he'd left off. His tongue and mouth played a cruel game of tag, retreat, and attack again until Tess shook with built-up tension.

"Let go, my darling. Let me take you over."

His words were the final stroke she needed. She gasped out his name as waves of pleasure washed over her.

Pushing her eyelids open was a struggle, but it was so worth the effort as it brought the sexiest man she'd ever known into view. He removed his shirt, providing her with a delicious view of his broad shoulders and wide, muscular chest that tapered down at the waist to a set of perfect hips. She absolutely loved the smattering of his chest hair, especially the arrow that shot from his naval to his...oh my. She blew out a long breath.

"You like something you see?" Kyle asked with a self-satisfied grin.

She held up her arms. "What I want is way too far away."

He chuckled and opened the drawer in the bedside table. An open box of condoms set next to a loaded Smith & Wesson forty-five.

"How could I not fall in love with a woman who keeps her condoms next to her gun?"

"Well, that's so if I'm disappointed, we can either try again or I can politely ask you to leave."

He laughed and opened a condom to roll on himself.

"Wait," she said. "Don't I get to have a little fun before the...um, main event?"

He shook his head. "Sorry, babe. I have almost no control left."

"Great. I love it fast and hard." She wiggled her fingers. "C'mon, big guy. Show me whatcha got."

"No pressure," he joked as he joined her on the bed.

The joking came to an abrupt halt as he took her into his arms and looked deeply into her eyes.

"I love you, Tess. I know you've never said those words to me, and that's fine. Know that I'll always be here for you."

He kissed her, and she felt his passion and love as it flowed from him in his touch. Her heart swelled until it felt as though it would explode in her chest. Elation and joy flowed through every cell. When he slipped inside her, she moaned her pleasure.

Her response seemed to be the encouragement he needed. He withdrew and plunged in again.

Her toes curled as an intense energy developed and moved like a tidal wave up from her feet and at the same time, down from her head. The two swells of powers met midway and exploded. Her orgasm hit her hard. She gasped and thrust her head hard against the mattress.

"Oh crap," he muttered. "I can't hold any longer."

He slammed into her, held tight against her as his cock jerked inside. His breathing came in pants and gasps as he lay on top of her.

"Sorry. Give me a minute and I'll move. I think you killed me."

Unwanted tears built and trickled from the corner of her eyes.

"Hey. What's this?" He brushed a tear from her temple. "Am I hurting you?" He began to move, but she wrapped her arms around him to hold him where he was.

She shook her head and sniffed. "It's just that...well...no one has ever made me feel the way you do."

He pulled her close. "Oh, babe. Nobody will ever love you like I do. Ever."

"I know. It's so hard for me."

"I understand. I really do. Lloyd hurt you. He stole everything good about love from you. Let me give that back to you."

She sniffed again. "I...I..." She hesitated, gathered her courage and said, "I love you, Kyle."

He kissed her softly. "I know, honey. Even when you didn't, I knew. We are meant to be together. Hell, I knew that back when you called me a red-necked Barney Fife."

"But I'm bringing so much grief down on you." She shook her head. "Your reelection signs are being destroyed. I'm driving a wedge between you and your brother. The horrible stories in the newspaper. You can do so much better than me."

"First, there is no one better than you, at least not for me. And second, everything you just said is total bull. The signs could be anything. Kids. Guys I've arrested. My opponent. And my brother? A wedge?" He chuckled and the vibration of it rattled from his chest into hers. "Honey, we're twins. You can't drive a wedge between us. My brother is stubborn and a lot of the time a complete jerk, but he's my brother." He kissed her. "I hate that he's making your life hard. Could be because he's jealous that I found the perfect woman."

She smiled. "Perfect woman? Have I met her?"

He wiped another tear away. "I don't know. Have you?. Dr. Sweeney? Have you met Dr. Sweeney? The most perfect woman in the world."

She punched his shoulder. "I'm not perfect."

"You are for me, Tess. You are for me."

His words were like cold water on a stinging burn.

"Thank you. You always know what to say."

"You know what I need now?" His stomach rumbled.

"I hear rumor there's a pizza in the kitchen."

"Meet you in two minutes," he said and kissed her. He slipped from the bed and went into the bathroom to take care of the used condom.

After grabbing her robe off a chair in the corner, Tess padded to the kitchen and sliced the now-cold pizza into slices. She added four to a plate and popped it in the microwave.

A pair of warm, male arms wrapped around her from behind.

"Hurry," she whispered. "My man will be out of the bathroom any minute."

Kyle chuckled. "Your man is out of the bathroom now."

She leaned back and rested on his chest. "You're a hell of man, Sheriff Monroe."

"Perfect for you?"

Turning to face him, she kissed him. "Perfect."

The microwave dinged, and Tess pulled the hot slices out.

"What do you want to drink? Iced tea? Coke? Water?"

"Tea is fine. I'll get some for both of us."

Tess settled on the couch with two plates and napkins. Kyle joined her carrying two glasses of iced tea with a piece of cold pizza gripped between his teeth.

"Cold pizza?"

He handed her a glass and removed the slice. "I'll eat pizza of any temperature short of frozen."

She rolled her eyes.

"Now, I need to talk to you," he said, dropping on the cushion beside her.

"What?" She took a bite and moaned a little. All meat pizza was one of her weaknesses.

"What are you doing this Sunday?"

She shrugged. "Hospital rounds. Maybe working in my sad flower garden. Why?"

"I want to take you to lunch at my parents' house."

Her stomach flipped at the idea. Meeting his parents right now while she was under attack in the newspapers was a horrible idea. She stalled, trying to figure out how to say no without offending him. "Your parents?"

"I do have parents, you know."

"No. I guess I didn't know. I mean, sure, of course you have parents. I didn't realize they were here. Somewhere I got the idea that your parents lived in Dallas or Whispering Springs, or Tyler, not Diamond Lakes."

"Nope. They live here."

"I guess since Troy was the only one I met during your surgery, I somehow made the jump to they don't live here."

"Makes sense. Actually, they were out of the country at the time. Roger had taken Mom on an anniversary cruise out of Prague. Troy kept them in the loop on how I was doing."

She nodded. "I see. Well, I appreciate the invite, but no. This is a horrible time to meet your parents."

"And the rest of the family," he added.

"I know Troy," she said with a scoff.

"And apparently you know my brothers too."

Frowning, she said. "Who?"

"Heath and Beau Rowland."

"Are your brothers? But...but...their last night is Rowland."

"As is my mothers. My dad died when Troy and I were six months old. Mom married Roger the following year and they had three children."

"Wow." She sagged against the couch. "I'm surprised. Rowland Ranch belongs to your family."

He nodded. "It does. Will you come?"

She shook her head. "No. I'm sorry but it would be awkward. Troy is not my biggest fan, and I'm assuming he'll be there?"

"I can tell him not to come."

"Oh, Kyle." She leaned forward to kiss him. "No. You cannot tell your brother not to come to his own parents' house. And thank you for wanting to take me but not right now. When the Lloyd situation dies down, maybe but not now."

She could only imagine the nightmare of sitting a table with Kyle's family while Troy sent nasty digs at her.

"I'm not going to give up. I know my family will love you as much as I do."

"Except Troy."

Kyle scoffs. "He's just jealous. Trust me. He'll come around."

———

SATURDAY MORNING, Tess woke with the hot, naked flesh of man pressed into her back, a thick arm with a sprinkling of dark hair flung over her waist. An alien sensation rippled through her. Her first thought was *I feel safe*, but that wasn't it. She didn't need a man to make her feel safe. Growing up without parents and moving from foster home to foster home, she'd learned to depend on no one but herself. She pulled herself out of the deep rut that was her life, worked her way through college and med school with a ton of menial jobs and a ton of loan debt.

No, it wasn't safety, per se. It was even a more foreign emotion. She felt loved. Kyle had always been open with his feelings. Her? Not so much. The last time she'd jumped into love, it'd been with Preston and look how that had turned out.

But her relationship with Kyle was different in so many ways, the first one being how long they'd known each other before their first kiss. A smile crept onto her lips. A kiss? Ha. She'd have rather kicked his ass than kiss him back then. Now, he filled a hole in her heart and in her life that she hadn't even known existed. No matter how many times she'd sent him away or tried to distance her problems from him, he wouldn't let go. Yes, she was loved and cherished, and with her life history, she was grabbing on to the feeling. How long it would last was anyone guess. It was almost impossible to imagine anyone loving her for more than a few months, but it sure seemed as though he was in this for the long haul.

"Stop thinking so loud," he grumbled. "Hard for a man to sleep."

"You awake?"

"I wasn't. I am now." He kissed her behind her ear. "What are you doing up so early? Wait, what time is it?"

"Early. Almost six. I need to get to the hospital soon."

He groaned.

"But you don't have to get up with me. Stay here and get some sleep. It was a, um, busy night."

With a chuckle, he asked, "Busy night? Is that what the kids are calling multiple rounds of fantastic sex?"

She bumped him with her ass.

"Do that again and you'll be mighty late to work."

She bumped him again.

He'd been right. She was over two hours late doing her rounds.

When she got home, Kyle was gone, but there was a large bouquet of flowers sitting on her living room coffee table. There was a note attached that simply read, *All My Love*.

Pressing the card against her chest, she couldn't contain the wide smile on her face. Kyle was not her first boyfriend, or even her first lover. However, he was the first man that wanted to take her home to meet his parents.

She found that both thrilling and terrifying.

CHAPTER TWELVE

Sunday morning, Preston Lloyd woke and found himself in an empty bed, which wasn't a new event in his life. Since Hunter's death, Constance had been sleeping in the guest room. He stretched his arms over his head. It was amazing how well he slept when he had the bed to himself.

After shaving and bathing, he dressed and went downstairs to see what their housekeeper had prepared for breakfast. He'd love to complain to his wife about the expense of a fulltime live-in cook slash maid, but Constance was a horrible cook and even worse housekeeper. For him, a house was only a home when it was clean and dinner was on the table when he got home. He wished he'd known all that about Constance before he'd married her.

Once he'd finished his usual breakfast of black coffee, orange juice, eggs over easy, and toast with a smidge of blackberry jam, he took his copy of the Sunday morning newspaper to his office. He sat his favorite leather recliner and popped the paper open. The headline almost made him lose his breakfast.

Local Doctor Cleared of All Charges

Damn. Double damn. How could people be so stupid as to not see Tess Sweeney's malpractice? She was going to be a thorn in his side forever, but especially during his run for the governorship. The last thing he needed was for her to sell the story of their affair to some tabloid. He had to do something about her while he could.

He placed a call to the other problem that had to be dealt with. Two birds. One stone.

"Hello?" Candy asked in a breathless tone.

"Hey, darling. I know it's early, but I can't get you out of my mind."

"Hold on a sec."

He heard a door close before Candy's whispery voice came back on the line. "Good morning, sweetheart. I was just thinking about you. It's so good to hear your voice. You've made my day. Any chance you might be able to get away for a couple of hours?" She giggled. "I've already told Roy I'm going shopping this afternoon, so name the place."

Her giggle was pure fingernails on a blackboard. He winced.

"Oh, honey. I wish I could. Constance is having one of her meltdowns today. I'm afraid I'll have to stay here. You know how unpredictable she is." He lowered his voice. "But I'd do just about anything to be with you. I can't wait for the day when we are together. Just you and me. When I run for governor, you're the wife I want beside me. If only I'd met you before Constance." He gave a dramatic sigh. "If only..."

"What? If only what?"

He sigh again. "I can handle Constance. It's Tess Sweeney who's becoming a real problem."

"What? What has she done now?"

"You mean besides kill my son? I'm sorry. I shouldn't

unburden myself on you like this, but you're the only person I've got in my corner. You are the only one who truly understands me and loves me."

"Of course I do. I'll always be here for you. Tell me what I need to do. You want me to talk to Roy about firing her?"

"I wish it were that simple. She's been calling me day and night wanting to get back together. I've tried telling her it's over and that I've moved on, but I'm afraid she's going to harm herself."

"Oh, no. That would be horrible for the hospital."

The hospital. Idiot woman. Who cared about the hospital?

"Did you see the article in today's paper?"

"I've only read the sale ads. Why? What's there?"

For a brief moment, he really wanted to bang his head on the wall. She might be great in bed, but the woman was interested in shopping and that was about it.

"It was about Tess and the problem she had with alcohol."

Among other things. Actually, the article had been about how Tess had turned her life around and all the volunteer work she did in the community. A real puff piece.

"That's awful," Candy said. "Roy won't be happy about that."

"I know," he said, his voice taking on the tone he used when trying to sway jurors. "Look, I have an idea, but I don't want to talk about it just yet. Can you meet me tomorrow morning? About ten?"

"Anything for you. Where?"

"I'll text you the location in the morning, okay?"

"Sure. Love you."

"Love you, precious."

He almost gagged at his own words.

Okay, he had his first fish on the line. Now to make sure he reeled her in.

In the meantime, he turned on his computer and began composing the sad, final letter from Tess Sweeney explaining why she'd killed Preston's lover and then herself.

At nine-thirty Monday morning, he sent Tess Sweeney's home address to Candy's phone.

Meet me at this address at 10. Park on the street.

Candy responded.

Whose address is this?

Preston rolled his eyes with an exasperated sigh. Stupid bitch with her stupid questions.

"A friend's house. See you at 10."

Preston pulled into Tess's driveway at nine-forty-five. One thing about Tess was that she was a creature of habit. As he'd expected, he found the front door key under the rabbit planter in her flower bed. After slipping on a pair of gloves, he let himself inside and the opened the garage door. He parked inside the garage and lowered the door. He didn't needed a nosy neighbor wondering about a strange car in Tess's driveway.

It didn't take more than three minutes to find Tess's gun. Right side of the bed, as usual. The Smith & Wesson was fully loaded, which was perfect. Her fingerprints would be on the bullets. Once Candy got here, he could make sure all traces of him were erased from her phone.

The sound of a car door closing grabbed his attention. He shoved the gun into his jacket pocket and hurried to the front door to wave Candy inside.

"Is this Tess Sweeney's house?" Candy asked, looking around. "What are we doing here?"

"Come here. I want to show you something."

He took Candy's arm and led her to the living room.

"Stay here," he said. "I wanted a witness. I'm going to take Tess's gun so she can't hurt herself."

"You are such a good person," Candy cooed.

Preston walked into the bedroom door and turned. He pulled the gun from his pocket and shot Candy in the chest.

She gasped, shock covered her face. "Pres..." She crumpled to the floor.

A second shot rang out, catching Preston in the back. Fire and pain like he'd never felt arced through him. He tried to raise the gun he was holding, but it'd fallen to the floor.

"What?"

"That's for being such a lying, cheating spouse."

His wife walked to stand in front of him, then kicked the Smith & Wesson across the room. The next shot hit him in the groin.

"That's for killing our son, you alcoholic bastard."

Preston toppled to the floor, gasping to draw in a breath. She put the barrel of the gun to his forehead.

"And this is from my Uncle Vincent."

Constance Theresa Longinotti Lloyd dropped the gun on the bed followed by an envelope. She exited through the back door, walked to her car parked a couple of streets over, drove to the Diamond Lakes Regional Airport and boarded the helicopter waiting for her. Forty-five minutes later, she boarded the private jet her uncle had sent to bring her home to Italy.

———

IF THERE WAS EVER a day Tess was glad was over, it would be today. Sunday's article had turned on the floodgates for phone calls and personal messages. Of course, there were a few negative ones but the vast majority were positive and supportive.

The surgery schedule was blown to smithereens by a

two-car accident. Two patients ended up in her care, but both surgeries were noneventful and routine, exactly like she liked them. Her other surgeries were bumped back on the schedule and she spent the entire day in the operating room.

When she turned onto her street, the first thing she noticed was a strange Mercedes Benz coupe parked in front of her house. Mercedes Benzes weren't unusual in Diamond Lakes, but finding one at her house was. The second shock came when she opened the garage door. Preston Lloyd's Range Rover was parked in her spot. She had no idea what was going on but she was sure she wasn't entering her house with Kyle or one of his guys going with her.

She pulled into her neighbor Connie's drive and pulled her cell from her bag to call Kyle.

"Kyle Monroe."

His deep baritone voice sent shivers down her spine.

"Hey. It's me."

"What's up, me?" His voice had a teasing tone.

"Something odd at my house."

"What going on?" All business now.

"I'm not sure. Preston Lloyd's SUV is in my garage and there is a strange car parked in front of my house. Can you send somebody?"

"Do not go in that house until I get there. You hear me, Tess?"

"I hear you. I'm parked at Connie's house and you don't have to worry. I'm not moving."

Within five minutes, two deputy patrol cars came to a screeching halt at her address. She got out to meet the deputies at the top of her drive.

"Sheriff Monroe said for us to wait for him, ma'am."

"No problem. I'm in no hurry."

Kyle roared up a couple of minutes behind his deputies.

"Who does that car belong to?" he shouted as he exited his own SUV.

One of the deputies read from the notebook in his hand. "Candace Kennedy McCall."

"Candy McCall? Why would she be at my house?" Tess asked.

"You stay here," Kyle said to Tess. "Men, let's move in."

Kyle shoved her front door open. "Sheriff's department," he shouted. "Come out with your hands up."

He motioned one of the deputies through the door. From her position in the street, Tess could hear the men shouting, identifying themselves and then she finally heard, "All clear."

Kyle waved her to the door.

"I want to make sure. You haven't been in here, right?"

"Right." She leaned around him trying to see inside. "What's going on?"

"We've got two dead bodies. Candy McCall and Preston Lloyd."

"What? No way. Let me see."

He caught her as she tried to pass him. "You probably don't want to go in."

"Like hell I don't."

"Tess, stay out here. I've called for the state police since it's Lloyd again."

"But how? Why?"

"I don't know but don't worry." He hugged her. "I'll get to the bottom of this."

———

THE NEXT COUPLE of days were exhausting. Print, digital and television reporters invaded the small community of Diamond Lakes talking to anyone and everyone who would stand still.

Tess was allowed into her house long enough to pack a bag—under state police supervision. Reporters shoved microphones in her face at home and at work, even though she repeatedly told them she knew nothing about what happened.

By the end of the week, the state police released her house back to her, not that she had any intention of sleeping there ever again. She wasn't superstitious in the least, but the idea of closing her eyes near the spot where Preston had died wouldn't be happening.

On Monday, a week after the shootings, she got a text from Kyle.

CAN YOU COME BY THE OFFICE THIS AFTERNOON? ABOUT 4?

DEPENDS. IS THIS SHERIFF MONROE MAKING THE REQUEST OR MY BOYFRIEND WANTING TO FOOL AROUND?

There was a long pause before he replied.

STILL TRYING TO DECIDE ANSWER TO YOUR QUESTION.

She laughed.

SEE YOU AT 4.

She was about five minutes early and the clerk told her to go on back. She knocked and walked in. Shade Gruber, a lieutenant with the state police who she'd met the previous week during the investigation, sat in one of the chairs.

"I'm sorry. I didn't know you have someone in here. I'll wait until you're done."

"No, no. Come on in, Tess. Gruber is here to talk to both of us."

"Oh, okay. Lieutenant Gruber. Nice to see you again."

Gruber shook her hand. "You too, Dr. Sweeney."

Tess took the seat next to Gruber. "What's up?"

"We're closing the investigation into Lloyd's death," Gruber said. "There'll be a press conference tomorrow, but I thought you deserved to hear our findings first hand."

She nodded. "Okay. Shoot." She winced. "Bad choice of words. Sorry."

Gruber chuckled. "From the evidence found on the scene as well as in Lloyd's house, we are pretty sure his plan was to shoot Mrs. McCall and frame you."

"That's insane," she replied.

Gruber nodded. "Seems like Lloyd had been acting strangely since the death of his son. He blamed you for that and wanted to make sure you paid."

"And Lloyd? Who shot him?"

"His wife."

"Constance? I would have never thought she had it in her. Why my house?"

"I think it was a matter of time and place. She'd installed an app on her phone that routed a copy of all her husband's texts to her phone. From the letter she left behind, she blames her husband for the death of their son. He'd been driving drunk and crossed the centerline. She might have been able to tolerate his numerous affairs but the death of her son seems to have tipped the scales for her."

"Have you found Constance yet?"

"Nope, and I doubt we ever will. We've traced her to a private plane that left Dallas shortly after she shot Lloyd. We're pretty sure she's gone to Italy. She has family there, family that's well-known within the organized crime community."

"I guess, for her, she got Texas justice for her son."

"Probably."

"So it's over?"

"As far as we are concerned. Constance Lloyd shot her husband. Preston Lloyd shot Mrs. McCall. Lloyd was responsible for the death of his son. That about sums it up," Gruber said.

"Appreciate your stopping by and filling us in," Kyle said.

Gruber stood. "Glad to." He held out his hand. "Let's get together for dinner soon."

Kyle shook his hand. "I'll look forward to it."

After Gruber left, Tess and Kyle stared at each other.

"It's over," Tess said. "Really over."

"Yep. That chapter of your life is closed. Hell, we'll call it that book. Slam the cover shut and toss it away. It's time to start a whole new book."

She laughed. "Sounds like a great idea."

"Great. I have another one."

"Idea?"

"Yeah." Kyle unlocked the bottom drawer of his desk. He pulled out a black velvet box and popped open the lid. "This is my idea." He walked around his desk, the obscenely large diamond in the ring catching the late afternoon sun. "We start the next book in your life together."

Tess felt her mouth gape. "Kyle?"

He took the seat that Gruber had vacated. He turned her chair until they were facing each other.

"Marry me, Tess. You can't be surprised. You know how I feel about you. I love you. You love me. I want to spend the rest of my life loving you."

Her vision became watery as tears built. "Are you sure, Kyle? You know the odds of my having children are not good."

"Don't care if we have kids, adopt kids or never have children. What I know is that without you, my life will be less that it could be." He pulled the ring from the box and slid it on her finger. "Okay?"

She smiled. "Okay."

He leaned forward and kissed her.

"Hey, Sheriff." Deputy Anderson's head popped through Kyle' ajar door. "There's a three-car pileup on Route Seventy. Oops. Sorry."

Kyle rested his forehead on Tess's. "New book. Page one. Romantic hero pulled away by work."

Tess laughed. "Go. We'll celebrate at home later."

"Love you."

"I love you too."

After Kyle left, Tess studied the ring on her finger. On the darkest night of her life in Memphis, the night her precious baby died, she'd believed she'd never find joy again. Now, such joy filled her soul, she felt like she would explode.

She gathered her things to head home when her phone rang.

"Dr. Sweeney," she answered.

"Hi, Dr. Sweeney. This is Martha from the ER. There's a three-car accident with injuries. Dr. Monroe is in house and asked that you come in."

"On my way."

No matter what fate threw at her, she knew she'd never have to face it alone. She smiled. It might have taken her thirty-four years, but she'd met her soulmate in Kyle Monroe. Her new ring sparkled, just like her future.

Look for these other books by Cynthia D'Alba

Whispering Springs, Texas

Diamond Lakes, Texas

Arkansas Mavericks

TEXAS TWO STEP

Whispering Springs, Texas Book 1 ©2012

The woman stood on tiptoe in the baggage-claim area of the Dallas/Fort Worth airport looking for all the world like someone who'd been sent to collect the devil. Mitch Landry had expected Wes or one of the other groomsmen to come for him. Instead, his gaze found a statuesque blonde arching up on her toes, a white T-shirt with Jim's Gym in black script stretched across her lushly curved breasts and long tanned legs extending from tight denim shorts. His heart stumbled then roared into a gallop.

Blood rushed from his brain to below his waist. His nostrils flared in a deep breath, as though he could smell her unique fragrance across the crowded lobby.

She hadn't looked in his direction yet, which gave him an unfettered opportunity to study her without having to camouflage his reactions.

No make-up covered her creamy rose complexion, not that she needed any. Not then and not now. No eye shadow was required to bring out the deep blue of her eyes. Nor did her mouth need any enhancement. Her lips radiated a natural pink, although the bottom one grew redder as her upper teeth gnawed on it.

Six years had passed since he'd seen Olivia Montgomery, but he'd swear she was more beautiful today. She had an appeal that came only with age and maturity. A smile edged onto his mouth. He was surprised—pleasantly surprised—to admit how glad he was to see her.

He watched as her glare bounced around the room, searching faces until it fell on him. As a look of resignation flashed across her face, she frowned.

His smile faded. Not exactly the reaction he'd hoped for.

TEXAS LULLABY

Whispering Springs, Texas Book 7

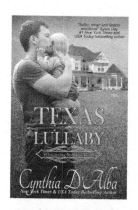

"I'm worried about my sister. She and Jim should be here by now."

As always, the sound of his fiancée's voice made Jason Montgomery's heart swell with love. He leaned over and put his arm around the back of her chair. "I'm sure they are just running behind schedule. It was probably tough for Meredith to get her and Jim and those three kids packed and on the road."

Lydia Henson rested her head on Jason's shoulder, tiny wisps of her brunette hair tickling his cheek. The scent of lilacs and lavender from her perfume swirled around him. He inhaled, letting the intoxicating aroma fill his lungs.

"You're probably right." Lydia chuckled. "Between my sister's kids and all the Montgomery children, there are going to be a lot of short people running around at our wedding tomorrow."

The excitement in her voice when she spoke of children drove a stake into his gut. By accepting his marriage proposal, she'd accepted not having a family. His adamant stand of not wanting children was a well-known fact, and something that wouldn't change.

"And that doesn't bother you?" he asked.

"What? Rumbustious kids at our wedding and reception? Of course not." She looked into his eyes. "I love my nieces and nephew. And I adore all the ones on your side. But you and I aren't cut out to be parents, and I've accepted that. I knew when we started dating that you didn't want children. And I appreciate your being so bluntly honest about it. The long and short of it is I'd rather spend my life with you and no children than spend my life with anyone else...period."

"I love you." He leaned in to kiss her but was interrupted by someone banging on a water glass with a knife. Resting his forehead on hers, he sighed and then looked in the direction of the noise. Dressed in a gray suit with a blue tie, his brother, Travis, stood directly in front of the head table where Jason and Lydia were sitting, a wide grin splitting his face.

Travis lifted his water glass. "To my brother and his soon-to-be wife. Caroline and I wish you all the happiness we've found."

Twenty glasses filled with wine, water or iced tea were lifted in a salute, along with shouts of well-wishes.

Cash, Jason's youngest sibling, stood. "I second that. And I have to say, it's about time you made an honest man out of my brother, Lydia."

Jason playfully elbowed Lydia. "Yeah."

Lydia laughed along with the rest of the Montgomery clan, as well as her parents. At three years, it had been a long engagement.

SADDLES AND SOOT

Whispering Springs, Texas Book 8 ©2015 Cynthia D'Alb

A grass fire can singe more than just the lawn.

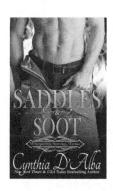

Veterinarian Georgina Greyson will only be in Whispering Springs for three months covering for the town veterinarian while he is on a research trip. She isn't looking for love or roots, just maybe a good time before she moves on.

When his parents leave on their dream fantasy RV trip, Tanner Marshall is left in charge of his family's cattle ranch, as well as his two younger brothers and sister. When he isn't ranching, he's doing duty on the volunteer fire department, a job he loves more than ranching. At thirty-four, he's ready to put down some roots, including marriage, children and the white picket fence.

When Georgina accidentally sets her yard on fire during a burn ban, the volunteer fire department responds and she gets quite the fire lecture from one very cute firefighter. If there's one thing Tanner hates, it's carelessness with fire, but there's something about his latest firebug that he can't get out of his mind.

Can an uptight firefighter looking to settle down convince a cute firebug to give up the road for a house and roots?

Whispering Springs, Texas, Book 8

The scent of smoke filtered around the side of the house. "I guess I'd better check on my fire."

"Your what?" Magda shouted. "Fire? Your house is on fire?"

"No, no. Nothing like that. I was burning trash, and a few things that needed to be permanently disposed of."

"There's a burn ban on right now. County's as dry as I've ever seen it. You might want to go put that fire out pronto."

"Burn ban? Seriously? I didn't know. I'll–"

The sound of a siren interrupted her. "I hear a siren close by. Guess you're probably right about putting out the fire. Holler at you later."

The smoke rolling around from the back of the house was heavier and darker now. Probably those darn running shoes smoldering. Maybe she should have thrown those into a Salvation Army bin. Too late now.

She screwed the hose nozzle onto the faucet at the side of the house and dragged the hose around to douse the fire. The unexpected heat from the growing blaze pushed her back. Somehow the fire had jumped its rock boundary and was eating its way toward the house.

Crap, crap, crap.

She'd begun frantically spraying the hose when a large, red firetruck braked to a stop in front of her house. Three men in tan turnout coats and pants jumped from the truck and scrambled for equipment. Behind the fire engine, five trucks skidded to a stop, red strobe lights on the dashes flashing through the windshields.

"Grab the hose and let's get it around back," the tall man from the first pickup truck shouted. "Buddy, be sure to get the fitting tight this time. We need all the water we can get." He shoved past Georgie with a gruff, "Move, lady."

Two firemen raced past her dragging a large hose toward her fire. Good grief. It wasn't even that big of a fire. Sure, it'd gotten out of its assigned location but she could have handled it with a simple garden hose. What an overreaction. Typical small volunteer fire department.

As that thought crossed her mind, the pine tree close to her bedroom window crackled as fire leapt up into its branches.

The animals! She needed to make sure they were okay.

Whirling around, she raced around the front of the house and approached the shared pasture from the other side of the house. Surprisingly, she found three more firemen there putting out small fires that'd started in the dead grass in the yard.

Running past them, she got to the fence and saw all three animals watching the firemen with a mixture of curiosity and fear. None of the burn paths had led to the pasture, so none of the animals she'd been trusted to protect were at risk. Even the smoke wasn't as thick over here.

The volume of water the firemen's hose sprayed was much greater than anything she could have generated with her garden hose. Within fifteen minutes, the fire was out and the men were rolling up their hose to leave.

A pain in the patoot for sure, but no real harm done.

The tall man who'd rudely shoved her out of the way stalked toward her with long strides and heavy footsteps.

"Lady," he said, his face red with either heat exposure or anger.

Georgie crossed her fingers for heat exposure. She was wrong.

"Are you nuts or stupid?" the man shouted. "You don't look crazy, so I'm going with stupid. There's a fire ban right now. That means *no fires*. At all. For any reason." He jerked the helmet off his head. Dark wavy hair fell over his forehead. "Well?" he demanded. A pair of chocolate brown eyes glared at her.

"Well, what?"

"Are you crazy or stupid?"

Georgie cocked her fists on her hips and widened her stance, hoping she looked intimidating. Sometimes that worked with her patients. Not with this guy.

"I'm neither, thankyouverymuch. I just got into town. I didn't know about the burn ban. Sorry. It wasn't part of the orientation to my house." She waved her hand toward the white clapboard house, as if he wouldn't know which house she was talking about. "Besides, no real harm done. I'm sure I could have put it out with a garden hose."

The man was a good six inches taller than she, and he took advantage of that stature to lean over her. "You know how a big fire gets started? With a small one. Yours would have spread fast if someone hadn't seen the smoke rising and contacted us. And ignorance of the ban is no excuse. Any person with a modicum of intelligence would have noticed the parched grass and dying trees around them. Get some glasses, lady, if you can't see that."

Ire rumbled in her gut. Standing on her tiptoes, she poked her finger into his chest, which was akin to poking the butcher block countertop in the kitchen. Dadgum near broke her finger. "I'm not stupid. And I'm not blind. And I'm sorry."

She dropped down off her toes. "Thank you for showing up. Am I going to get a fine?"

The corners of his mouth twitched as though he might smile, but the movement went no further. "That'll be up to Sheriff Singer, but he's a good guy. He might go easy on you if you explain." His sexy chestnut eyes squinted into a serious expression. "No matter where you live, *always* check with the fire department before you burn."

She stepped back and saluted. "Yes, sir."

That did produce a tiny smile. The man turned on his boot heel and headed back to the truck. With engines growling, all six vehicles roared back down her drive to the highway. There, they went in separate directions.

She'd never experienced a volunteer fire department response. Interesting would be one word to describe it.

And the head of the response? He'd be best described as intriguing.

New York Times and *USA Today* Best-selling author Cynthia D'Alba started writing on a challenge from her husband in 2006 and discovered having imaginary sex with lots of hunky men was fun. She was born and raised in a small Arkansas town. After being gone for a number of years, she's thrilled to be making her home back in Arkansas living in a vine-covered cottage on the banks of an eight-thousand acre lake.

Photo by Tom Smarch

When she's not reading or writing or plotting, she's doorman for her two dogs, cook, housekeeper and chief bottle washer for her husband and slave to a noisy, messy parrot. She loves to chat online with friends and fans.

You can find her most days at one of the following online homes:

Website: cynthiadalba.com

Facebook:Facebook/cynthiadalba

Twitter:@cynthiadalba

Blog:Cynthia's World

Drop her a line at cynthia@cynthiadalba.com

Send snail mail to: Cynthia D'Alba PO Box 2116 Hot Springs, AR 71914

Or better yet! She would for you to take her newsletter. She promises not to spam you, not to fill your inbox with advertising, and not to sell your name and email address to anyone. Check her website for a link to her newsletter.

Reviews? She loves them! The best way you can help an author is to buy books and leave reviews. So want to help? Review please!

Want more sizzling, western romance from *New York Times* bestselling author Cynthia D'Albaz?

Read on for excerpts from her other books!

Made in the USA
Coppell, TX
01 July 2021

58416342R00075